Paige was in need of rescue—

rescue from the wild impact Zach's casual touch had on her body. "Well," she said, struggling to regain some degree of aplomb, "Jessie and I will get busy with our lesson and you can come back in an hour."

"I think I'll stay and watch awhile."

"Watch?"

"I promise not to be a distraction."

He already was, Paige thought, as he leaned his very-male body back against the piano.

Zach felt more like he'd be the one distracted as a wafting tendril of Paige's sexy scent drifted toward him. Something feminine and outrageously provocative—like the woman wearing it....

Dear Reader,

As Celebration 1000! moves into its third exciting month, Silhouette Romance is pleased to present a very special book from one of your all-time favorite authors, Debbie Macomber! In *The Bachelor Prince,* a handsome prince comes to America in search of a bride to save his country from ruin. But falling for the wrong woman made his duty a struggle. Was loving Hope Jordan worth losing his kingdom?

If you enjoyed Laurie Paige's WILD RIVER books in the Special Edition line, don't miss *A Rogue's Heart,* as Silhouette Romance carries on this series of rough-and-ready men and the women they love.

No celebration would be complete without a FABULOUS FATHER. This month, Gayle Kaye tells the heartwarming story of a five-year-old ballerina-in-the-making who brings her pretty dance teacher and her overprotective dad together for some very private lessons.

Get set for love—and laughter—in two wonderful new books: *Housemates* by Terry Essig and *The Reluctant Hero* by Sandra Paul. And be sure to look for debut author Robin Nicholas's emotional story of a woman who must choose between the man she loves and the town she longs to leave in *The Cowboy and His Lady.*

Next month, the celebration continues with books by beloved authors Annette Broadrick and Elizabeth August. Thanks so much for joining us during this very special event.

Happy reading!

Anne Canadeo
Senior Editor

Please address questions and book requests to:
Reader Service
U.S.: P.O. Box 1325, Buffalo, NY 14269
Canadian: P.O. Box 1050, Niagara Falls, Ont. L2E 7G7

DADDY TROUBLE
Gayle Kaye

Silhouette
R O M A N C E™
Published by Silhouette Books
America's Publisher of Contemporary Romance

For my daughter, Cathy,
who learned to spread her wings
and fly. This one's for you, with love.

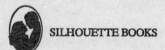 SILHOUETTE BOOKS

ISBN 0-373-19014-X

DADDY TROUBLE

Copyright © 1994 by Gayle Kasper

This edition published by arrangement with Harlequin Enterprises B.V.

® and TM are trademarks of Harlequin Enterprises B.V., used under
license. Trademarks indicated with ® are registered in the United States
Patent and Trademark Office, the Canadian Trade Marks Office and in
other countries.

Printed in U.S.A.

Books by Gayle Kaye

Silhouette Romance

Hard Hat and Lace #925
His Delicate Condition #961
Daddy Trouble #1014

GAYLE KAYE

had a varied and interesting career as an RN before finally hanging up her stethoscope to write romances. She indulges this passion in Kansas City, Missouri, where she lives with her husband and one very spoiled poodle. Her first romance in 1987 reached the finals of the Romance Writers of America Golden Heart contest.

When she's not writing, she loves to travel or just curl up with a good book.

Zach Delano On Fatherhood...

When I found myself raising my little girl alone, I was terrified at first. Dressing her, I was all thumbs, especially when tying pink bows in her hair. But we soon became good friends, pals, Jessie and I.

Jessie's mother died, so I became her mother as well as her father. I wasn't very good at the motherhood part, admittedly, but my love for Jessie, my determination to see her happy and healthy and safe made up for my inabilities.

Jessie was unsure of herself and her place in the world. I knew she felt different from other kids—maybe because she didn't have a mother, just an overprotective father, or maybe because she wore glasses. The pretty pink frames made her pixie face look adorable, I thought, but Jessie wasn't so sure.

It wasn't long before I realized my daughter needed more than I could give her, such as a few of the feminine graces. Enrolling her for dance lessons at Miss Paige's school seemed an ideal solution.

I had hoped that Paige Hanford could make a difference in my daughter's life, and she did . . . in a way I never expected.

Chapter One

"**O**kay, let's take it from the top again. Music."

The fast-paced musical beat filled the studio in the basement of Paige Hanford's house as twelve four-year-old girls tapped semigracefully across the floor. Or rather eleven did. The twelfth one had two left feet.

Paige tried to ignore the child's missteps and concentrate on the others in an effort to finish the number that they'd already run through two dozen times tonight. Several girls showed great promise, along with the enthusiasm and determination necessary to become accomplished dancers one day. They reminded Paige of her own talent at that tender age, and she smiled.

Just then, she heard a clatter and realized her ugly duckling had tapped to the left instead of the right,

knocking over a scenery prop for the upcoming recital, a giant tree that Paige had finished painting that
afternoon and had left drying in the corner.

The tree toppled as if felled by a crazy lumberjack,
and little Jessie Delano collapsed on top of it. Eleven
girls tittered while Paige stared in horror.

"Jessie!" Paige raced to see if the girl was all right.
Leaf-green paint smudged the child's right cheek and
tree-trunk brown adhered to one knobby knee, but
other than that, she appeared to be unhurt. So was the
tree.

Paige breathed a sigh of relief.

"Jessie, honey, why don't you sit out awhile." She
quickly found the child a chair and waited until she
slid onto it. Jessie's pink lower lip puckered out in a
pout, which caused Paige more than a qualm or two
of guilt.

This had not been the first such mishap. The girl,
sweet though she was, lacked the coordination to
make it through a number all the way to the end, much
less become accomplished enough for Paige to put her
on stage in the recital less than two months away.

Paige knew what she had to do—and she didn't rel-
ish the task. She would have to tell the child's father
that his daughter had no talent for dance whatsoever
and that he was wasting his money on lessons for her.

From what Paige had seen of the man, she'd sooner
tango with the devil. A quick image of broad shoulders, dark hair and dangerous silver-gray eyes flashed
into her mind. Zach Delano would not be pleased that

she was sending his little princess packing, along with her tutu and slightly scuffed tap shoes, but it couldn't be helped.

Paige was in no position to lose even one student from her fledgling school, DanceWorks. This was her first season and she desperately needed to make it a success. Still, she couldn't, in all conscience, keep on a child with no aptitude for the art.

"All right, let's go, girls. One more time." She clapped her hands to get her Broadway babies, minus one, back into formation.

This time the number went off without a hitch and Paige gave a satisfied smile. After one more run-through, she dismissed the small troupe and went to check on Jessie.

The girl had been watching the others with a look of longing that tore at Paige's heart and threatened her resolve. It was for the child's own good, she rationalized. Next time she might seriously injure herself, and that was a risk Paige couldn't take.

"How's that knee?" she asked, rubbing at the smudge of tree paint clinging to it.

Jessie studied her reflection in her tap shoes and her lower lip puckered again, sending Paige's guilt-o-meter soaring off the scale.

A few of the mothers were beginning to arrive to pick up their children. Paige didn't allow anyone to sit in on the sessions, feeling that her young protégées did better without their parents in attendance. After meeting Zach Delano, she was glad it was a rule she adhered to. The big, sexy man unnerved her, more than she cared to admit.

She spoke to several of the mothers, giving them progress reports on their children. When she glanced up, she saw Zach standing in the doorway, his eyes scouring the room for his little darling. A smile edged his lips when he found her. The man doted on the girl. That was plain enough to see.

Paige squared her shoulders, preparing herself to face him. He crossed the room in long, powerful strides, eating up the distance from the door to where Paige stood beside his daughter. A shiver tap-danced down her spine and her mouth felt as if she'd swallowed dandelion fluff.

The man was good-looking in that male-confident sort of way, his face lean and ruggedly appealing, his lips sensually full. His hair was black and thick, curling over the collar of his leather bomber jacket. Beneath it, a black turtleneck stretched across his broad chest, and soft-worn jeans sheathed his long, muscular legs.

He offered her a quick nod, then turned to Jessie. "How did class go tonight, sugar?" he asked in a low rumble that brushed across Paige's nerve endings and made her wish he'd used the endearment on *her*.

Jessie looked up at him with big, soulful eyes and sniffed. "I knocked over a tree...*that* tree," she said, pointing to the offending structure she'd toppled earlier.

"She's quite all right," Paige inserted quickly to reassure him. "She didn't hurt herself." Then she glanced down at Jessie. "Honey, why don't you go and take off your tap shoes while I talk to your daddy."

Zach's eyes widened for a moment in surprise, then he ruffled Jessie's dark curls. "Do what Ms. Hanford tells you," he said.

When Jessie scampered off, he turned to Paige, jolting her with the full impact of his dangerous good looks. She swallowed against the dryness in her throat and rubbed her sweating palms down the sides of her black leotard. Did the man have to be so unsettling?

"Sit down, Mr. Delano," she said, indicating a bench against the wall.

He glanced at it, but made no effort to move toward it. "You can call me Zach," he said, as if that in itself were a special privilege.

Paige resisted using any name. In defiance? She wasn't sure. "I'd like to talk to you about Jessie."

"What about Jessie?" Alarm flared in his eyes.

Paige put a reassuring hand on his arm, then wished she hadn't. The man was all-too-male flesh and blood beneath her touch. Hard and firm and... She snatched back her hand and forced a faint smile, instead.

How was she ever going to explain? The man was so forbidding. And so protective of Jessie. If she said one word against the child, she was certain he'd take her to task for it. For a moment, she considered dropping the entire matter—but that was the coward's way out and she knew it. She stiffened her shoulders and began again.

"Jessie is not doing well in the class and—"

"What do you mean, she's not doing well?" His gaze was fierce, pinning her to the spot.

She sucked in a breath. "She just isn't...dancer material."

His lip curled. "After only three months you've decided that? I didn't expect her to be ready for the stage, Ms. Hanford. This is a kiddie class. You know, fun and enjoyment."

"I'm well aware of what this class is, but—"

"But what?" His stare was penetrating.

Paige refused to be intimidated by either his good looks or his infuriated gaze. She swallowed hard and began again. "To be blunt—Jessie is a klutz. She taps right when she should go left. Take that tree, for instance." She waved at the fallen prop in the corner, to which he granted a cursory glance. "She tries hard, but she ends up tripping over her own feet."

He gave her an indignant glower. "She's only four years old, for crying out loud. Give the kid a break."

Paige sighed. "I've tried to, believe me, but she's just not...coordinated. You'd do better to take the money you're putting into dance lessons and find something she's more suited to."

"I hardly need you to tell me where to put my money, Ms. Hanford."

Paige's jaw set. What had she expected from the man? He thought the sun rose and set on his daughter. She saw the way he looked at the child—as if she were a walking dream.

"Maybe Jessie needs a teacher with a little more patience and a little less in the expectations department," he remarked sharply.

What he said brought Paige up short for a moment. Had she been too critical of Jessie's performance? Had she not exercised enough patience with the girl?

Paige drew herself up to her full five-foot-two height. She was always patient, giving her full one hundred percent and then some, with every child under her tutelage. She loved working with the kids. And little Jessie was one of the dearest. But every child had his or her own niche, she knew, and this clearly wasn't Jessie's.

"Mr. Delano, I know how you feel but—"

"Do you now?" One dark eyebrow shot up, eloquently expressing his doubt about the matter. "I don't think you do. Or how Jessie will feel."

Paige wished he hadn't added the last. It was the part of all this she regretted the most. "Jessie will soon forget about this class and find something else she likes to do, something she's really *good* at. I do believe that—or I wouldn't be taking this step." She looked him squarely in the eye as she spoke the words, but it seemed to have little effect. No one hurt his child—and clearly that was the way he interpreted Paige's action. Hurtful.

"Would you like me to speak with her about it?" she asked as a final peace offering. "Perhaps I can soften the blow."

His stormy gray eyes turned thunderous. "I think you've done quite enough, thank you."

Paige opened her mouth to say something more—what, she wasn't entirely sure. She just didn't want to see things end this way. But at that moment, Jessie returned with her feet tucked into a pair of shiny black Mary Janes, cradling her tap shoes in her arms. On her nose sat a pair of small pink-framed glasses, the lenses magnifying her cornflower-blue eyes.

Paige knew Jessie stuffed them into her dance bag for class. And she also knew why. The little girl wanted to feel pretty while she danced. Paige could understand that. Little Jessie felt different.

And now Paige was going to make her feel even more so.

She swallowed a lump of regret. She felt like the world's worst heel, someone who kicked dogs and shoved little old ladies off sidewalks. She hoped Jessie would get over her disappointment quickly and find some new interest to catch her attention.

Tearing her gaze away from Jessie, she returned it to Zach. "I . . . I really am very sorry about this," she said, not knowing what else to offer.

He put up his hands to stop her words. His silver-gray eyes were as icy as a glacier, his tone just as cold. "Spare me the rhetoric—*please*." He snatched Jessie's jacket off the coatrack, then turned back to Paige. "Good night, Ms. Hanford."

Before Paige could even muster a goodbye to the child, he hustled Jessie out the door.

Paige stood there for a long, tortured moment after they left, hugging her arms to herself and staring at the empty doorway.

Right now she didn't like herself very much. But she'd done the right thing for Jessie—even if Zach Delano didn't agree.

She only hoped the girl didn't hate her for it.

With a slow, shuddering sigh, she began to straighten up the small studio.

Zach had promised himself he wouldn't do this. He wouldn't go anywhere near that woman again. She was one half-pint of trouble, with those sassy green eyes and uptilted nose. And that mouth—as ripe and full as a succulent cherry. He'd thought about the taste of it for days, wondering if it was tart like her attitude, or tasty sweet.

Forget it, Zach, he cautioned himself as he aimed his black Bronco toward Libertydale Park. Today was business, strictly business. One small meeting with the woman to discuss Jessie. He'd do anything for his daughter, even swallow his fury at Paige Hanford.

He'd set this meeting at the park rather than at her place, not so much because he wanted to meet her on neutral territory, but because, away from her studio, she wouldn't likely be dressed in that skinny black leotard that cupped every curve or those high-heeled tap shoes that accentuated the beautiful shape of her legs.

He'd had one hell of a time the other night keeping his mind on his anger, his righteous indignation, and off the woman in front of him. His libido had taken a direct hit—and it still hadn't fully recovered.

Yes, meeting at the park was a smart move. He congratulated himself on it as he wheeled the Bronco into the graveled parking lot. He was early, he knew, but he had nothing else to do. He hadn't been able to concentrate on a damn thing all day. And he placed the blame for that squarely on Paige Hanford's pretty little head.

He climbed out of the four-by-four, sauntered over to a picnic table and sat down, straddling the bench as he waited for her to show. The park was situated along the Missouri River, with a meandering jogging path parallel to its bank. This was where he often took his early morning run, outracing the Mighty Mo's fast current, drinking in nature's solitude. It was where he brought Jessie to play on cool summer evenings.

Jessie. He hadn't had the heart to tell her yet that Miss Paige—as her students called her—didn't want her in class, that she wouldn't get to wear a costume of sequins and glitter in the recital she'd been looking forward to. That she hadn't measured up to her teacher's *lofty* expectations. His teeth ground at the thought.

He could check out the other small dance academy in town. The teacher had impressive credentials—excellent in fact—but his daughter wanted Miss Paige. She was all Jessie talked about from morning till night. And if that was what she wanted, Zach intended to get it for her.

There were some who said he was an overprotective father, primarily his crotchety housekeeper, Ernestine. She also said that he spoiled the child. Well, if being sure she was safe, that no harm would ever befall her, that she was happy and secure, then he supposed he was guilty.

Jessie had been hurt enough in her young life—and he intended to make sure she never was again.

Paige jogged along the river trail, enjoying the afternoon sun that was surprisingly warm for early April. The breeze slapped against her face, pinkening her cheeks and cleansing her lungs. The river kept pace beside her, like a comfortable companion.

She didn't come here often, at least not as often as she'd like to. So much of the past year and a half had been devoted to getting DanceWorks off to what she hoped was a successful start.

Libertydale was home now. So was the red brick bungalow-style house she'd bought with the small inheritance left to her by her grandfather. It had been enough for a sizable down payment and a few modest renovations to the basement that had turned it into her very own dance academy.

The town had changed a lot since she'd left. She'd grown up here, gone to school here, taken dance in the old Majestic Theater building, now turned into a collection of trendy law offices. The town had expanded its city limits by a few housing developments and office parks. It was no longer small-town America, but it was still midwestern America, which she'd sorely missed the years she'd lived on the West Coast with her then husband.

But she didn't want to think about him right now. Or the sorry life they'd shared. Or the divorce that had left her exactly nowhere—and a nobody. Paige Prescott was now Paige Hanford. She'd taken back her own name, the name she'd started out life with. And she was fast becoming her own person once again.

She wasn't sure why she'd chosen to return to Libertydale. It had just seemed the best place to start life over. And she was doing just that. At the moment, there was only one thundercloud on her otherwise serene horizon.

And his name was Zach Delano.

As she neared the end of the jogging trail, she saw him, looming large and male and sensual as he paced beside one of the park's redwood picnic tables. But this meeting with the man would be no picnic. Of that, she was certain.

Why did he want to see her? If it was about Jessie, she thought she'd made things bluntly clear a few nights ago. She hadn't changed her mind about Jessie's potential as a dancer.

In addition, he was precisely the kind of man she'd vowed to stay away from, overbearing, overprotective and determined to have his way in this world. Paige was still working at becoming a strong person—independent, assertive—and men like Zach Delano ate women like her for lunch.

He was the new assistant district attorney in town, she'd learned from the mother of one of her students. Mimi, a tall, thin, chatty woman had hinted at some terrible tragedy in his life, a wounded soul yet unmended. Paige denied she'd been curious, much less besotted like Mimi, who gushed and made it clear she thought that tragedy made the man all the more intriguing.

No, Zach didn't affect her at all.

Swallowing the taste of that bitter lie on her tongue, she approached him. "Zach..."

Zach whirled around and found the woman he'd come to meet standing next to him. He'd been watching the parking area for her to arrive. He hadn't expected her to be jogging—jogging in garb every bit as seductive as what she'd had on in her studio the other night.

Tights in iridescent blue spandex stretched over her firm legs and even firmer derriere, doing little to hide her gorgeous shape, but rather enhancing it. Her feet were tucked into a pair of pink slouch socks and well-worn running shoes. A stretched-out purple sweatshirt swallowed up the top half of her, its nonshape skimming over her pert breasts and flirting with the rounded curve of her hips.

Zach swallowed hard. Once again he found himself trying to talk intelligently and logically to a woman who made him think only about how much he wanted to take her to bed.

"What did you want to see me about?" she asked as she did her cooling-down exercises, bending that enticing body in slow, sensual stretches in front of him.

Zach rubbed the back of his neck, wishing she'd stop, and afraid that she would, thus denying him the pleasure of watching her lithe body move with such poetry. Her hair swung in the same lyrical motion, tawny and thick and tied to one side in a loose ponytail.

"Have a seat," he said, his voice coming out more gruffly than he intended.

She sat on the bench. He sat on the table a few safe feet away from her, not trusting himself to get any closer. The woman affected him more than he cared to admit.

"Is this about Jessie?" she asked, looking up at him expectantly. "I suppose she was a little disappointed when you first told her—"

"I didn't tell her."

Her eyes widened in surprise, and something else—censure. "You...didn't...tell...her?"

He shifted uncomfortably under that green-eyed gaze as it speared through him. "I can't tell her. Jessie needs this class. I realize my daughter isn't the most graceful child in the world—"

"That's what I was trying to tell you the other night," she interrupted.

"Please..." He raised his hand to stop her words. "Hear me out."

"Look, Zach, I'm not likely to change my mind about this."

"Just listen, please."

She gave a weary sigh, but quietly complied.

"I realize my daughter isn't exactly Miss Graceful. I also know that she won't develop any poise or polish by only being around my arthritic housekeeper and me. Ernestine moves like a battleship in choppy seas, and I...well, I'm a man. I walk like one. I move like one."

He certainly did, Paige mused. With every male muscle. Her gaze slid over his six-foot frame. If those jeans fit any tighter, she'd worry about the inseams splitting. As it was, she had to wonder how there was room in those pockets for such essentials as car keys and a wallet. Dark, silken chest hair spilled through the V of his forest-green pullover sweater. And no doubt spread like velvet over a taut-muscled torso beneath.

Snagging back her gaze, as well as her healthy imagination, she returned her attention to the conversation. "Certainly there's some woman who can be an influence in Jessie's life."

She didn't want it to be her. She had her own agenda, her newly formed dance academy to get on its shaky toes, the new life she was forging for herself.

And she suspected the compellingly male, all-too-intriguing Zach Delano could be a threat to those plans. If she was wise, she'd keep her distance from him.

He levered himself off the picnic table and stood next to it, his long, lean body casting its shadow across her in the late-afternoon sun. "There's no one in my life at the moment," he said, his eyes shuttered from view. "Jessie's mother died a year ago. And Jessie's still trying to adjust."

He glanced at Paige then. She saw the emotion swimming in his eyes' gray depths and she couldn't remain unmoved. This was the tragedy in his life that Mimi had hinted at, what it was that had wounded his soul. Paige felt for him—and little Jessie.

"Please," he said. "I can't bear to turn Jessie's life upside down again by taking her to another school. Let her continue in the class. Don't take away a little girl's dream."

Paige looked away from him and hugged her arms to herself as she studied the bark on an old oak. She knew all about young girls' dreams. She'd had her own at Jessie's age. She'd wanted to dance ever since her parents had taken her to a production of the *Nutcracker* in nearby Kansas City. She'd wanted to be a graceful Snowflake, pirouetting across the stage in pale pink tights and a snow-white tutu.

Dance had always come easy to her. But it didn't to Jessie. "I...I have the other girls in the troupe to consider. I can't neglect them while I give Jessie more time . . . more attention." She hated herself for seeming so unfeeling to Jessie's special dream of being a beautiful dancer, but what she told Zach was the truth.

"Then teach Jessie separately, a special class. I'd pay extra for your time, of course." A hopeful smile edged his firm, hard mouth. She suspected he didn't smile often, but when he did, it was an event. And made a woman want to see it again.

She wanted to see it again. "I suppose I could look at my schedule. It's not a matter of money—" although her struggling dance school needed every dime she could bring in "—but time. With the recital less than two months away, it's in short supply right now."

She didn't add that she worked odd jobs as well to help fund this first stage production. The fee she charged for classes helped defray the cost, but not entirely.

The smile broke across his face, wide this time, confident, like a man who'd gotten his way. "You won't regret this," he said. "Jessie will work hard. And . . . I'll even pitch in to help with the recital," he offered magnanimously. "It's the least I can do."

Oh, no, Paige thought, that would be all she needed. Not that she couldn't use his strong back transporting props and setting them up, or a myriad of backstage duties she still wasn't sure where she'd get the help to do. But not Zach, not this man whom she found entirely too disturbing to her senses.

"Thanks, but no thanks. I can handle the recital myself," she returned a tad sharper than she'd intended.

He gave her a studied glance for a moment. "If you say so," he said with a shrug of his wide shoulders. "Tell me when you want Jessie to come for her lesson and I'll have her there."

He and Paige set a time that was agreeable to both of them, then he turned to leave. A moment later, he spun back around. "Maybe I could, uh, sit in. On her class—you know, *watch*. I could observe the steps, help Jessie practice at home."

Paige hid a smile at the image of this big man learning the small, intricate steps of a tap number or attempting the graceful arabesque of a ballet. He'd be much more adept at dancing around a courtroom, intimidating witnesses.

She definitely did not want him coming as a package deal with Jessie.

She shook her head. "No. If I agree to work with Jessie, it will need to be strictly *one-on-one*."

She smoothed a hand over her leotard, then checked her hair for flying loose ends, hating herself for the gesture. She refused to admit that she'd been waiting all day for this moment, waiting to see Zach again. It was crazy—*she* was crazy. There was no other explanation for it.

She gave one last quick glance around the room, but there was nothing else she could busy herself doing. Nothing was out of place. The scenery props had been safely put out of range of flying feet. She could only stand there and wait until Zach came through the doorway.

Her heart skittered and she willed it into calm.

Jessie stumbled across the threshold ahead of her father, her little feet seemingly racing ahead of the rest of her until she fairly tumbled into the room.

"Jessie," Paige cried out and made a leap to grab her before the little girl fell. So did Zach, and in an instant they both had their arms in a tangle around her.

Jessie giggled and wiggled out of the huddle, which left Paige and Zach caught together, faces close, hands touching each other in sensually dangerous places. She could feel his warm breath against her right ear and she was certain she'd heard a clearly pleasurable *"Mmmmm"* coming from his very sexy mouth.

"You two look funny," Jessie said, as she giggled again.

Paige was definitely enjoying this momentary brush of nearness, but she began to see it from the perspec-

Chapter Two

Paige hurried about, straightening up the studio after the last Saturday-morning class. Zach would be arriving soon with Jessie for her first private lesson. She hoped she hadn't made a mistake agreeing to this arrangement.

She reached down and picked up a tap shoe that hadn't gotten stuffed into some child's dance bag and set it on a shelf where its owner would be sure to find it next time.

Just then, she heard the familiar metal creak of the storm door at the top of the stairway that led to her basement studio. Two sets of footsteps clattered down, one heavy, surefooted and male, the other small, soft and eager.

Zach and Jessie.

tive of a four-year-old—they must look very funny indeed.

"Excuse me," she said, removing one very masculine hand from its dangerous proximity to her right breast, and easing away from him. "It doesn't seem that Jessie's in dire need of rescue, after all."

Paige was the one in need of rescue at the moment—rescue from the wild impact Zach's touch had on her body. She ran nervous hands down the sides of her leotard, fingers spread and trembling, and took a shaky step or two back from the faint hint of a smile decorating his face.

"Well, now," she said, struggling to regain some degree of aplomb. "Jessie and I will get busy and you...you can come back in an hour."

She figured that was somewhat longer than the child's short attention span would hold, but right now she was more concerned with getting this man out of her domain.

But instead of heading for the door, he pulled out the piano bench and sat down. "I think I'll stay and watch awhile."

"Watch?"

"I promise not to be a distraction."

He already was, Paige thought, as he leaned his virile body against the piano she'd had since she was ten. She'd recently dragged it out of storage and set it up here to pound out dance tunes on. Now Zach looked as if he'd permanently staked his claim to it.

Zach felt more as if he'd be the one distracted as a wafting tendril of Paige's sexy scent drifted toward him. Something feminine and outrageously provocative, like the woman wearing it.

He remembered their agreement, that she would teach Jessie one-on-one. That meant no interference from him. And he didn't plan to cause any, but he did intend to exert more control over these lessons than he had in the past.

In the past, he'd complied with her request to scram, and the result had been the dismissal of his daughter from the woman's class. No. He wasn't about to leave and come back later.

He gave Paige a small half smile. "I'll be as quiet as the proverbial mouse."

A mouse was not the creature that came to mind when Paige thought of Zach Delano. He was more like a bull moose, and she was on the verge of telling him that when little Jessie interrupted.

"Want to see me do an *ara—arabesque?*"

Jessie had slipped out of her tennies and into her ballet slippers, and without waiting for permission to perform, awkwardly executed the step Paige had shown the class last week. Also gone were her pink-framed glasses.

Jessie was a princess when dancing—not a little girl in glasses. Paige smiled as she watched her pupil, Zach momentarily forgotten. Somehow she would make this work. And with the possible exception of one overbearing parent, she might not live to regret it.

* * *

Zach trained his gaze on Jessie as Paige led her through a few graceful bends and twists, standing at something called the *barre*, a wooden rail attached to a mirrored wall. Maybe he'd put up one at home for her, he thought. Paige could help him decide on the proper height.

He leaned back against the piano, pleased with himself that he had something he could do for his daughter. He loved Jessie. Nothing was too good for her. He beamed like a proud mother hen and watched as Paige and Jessie flitted across the floor in a simple little number—the *Dance of the Butterfly*.

The ballet—its movements, its imagery—had an exotic quality to it. Paige danced it with elegance, he thought, his gaze straying—not for the first time— from child to teacher.

Paige was no bigger than a minute, but in those stretchy black tights she looked as if she were all legs. Delectable legs. From the soles of her ballet slippers to...

He was supposed to be watching the dance, not the dancer, he remembered, taking his gaze off those enticing curves. But it would be a hell of a lot easier on his powers of concentration if Paige danced in something a little less formfitting. Like a tarp.

He was certain he could see the faint outline of one nipple under that shiny leotard, a pert nipple, all round and...

Agony. He was in agony. He shifted to a more comfortable position on the piano bench, wondering why it was so damned hot in here. He leaned back to rest his elbows and hit the keyboard, the unmelodious sound startling him as well as the two dancers.

Paige shot him a sharp glower for his offense, and Jessie giggled. "I thought you agreed to be quiet," Paige said, hands on hips.

"Sorry." He stood up. "I'll just, uh, walk around."

"Around the block maybe, but not around this room. We need the space—all of it."

He shrugged. "I'll stay out of your way. Promise." He strayed to the doorway and lounged against the jamb, arms folded over his chest, legs crossed at the ankle.

Paige gave a labored sigh in defeat. She doubted a female won often, if at all, in a confrontation with this man. As an assistant D.A. he was accustomed to exerting his power and influence in the courtroom. If he didn't have such a soft spot in his heart for little Jessie, he'd probably wield his power with her, too. He gave the child very little space as it was, planting himself firmly in her young life, dominating it.

Paige hadn't wanted him to stay and observe, she'd wanted to spend the full hour with Jessie, to let her learn to spread her wings—alone. Without Zach's presence.

This was why she didn't approve of parents staying to watch her classes. They distracted the children. But Zach distracted *her*.

She'd felt his heated gaze on her while she danced. She could feel it on her now, sliding over her like warm butter.

And she hated the fact that it excited her.

She'd spent the past year and a half recovering from a divorce and a marriage that had been male-dominated. She was—like Jessie—learning to spread her wings.

She'd married young, too young. She'd known very little about men then. But she did now. She knew the kind of man she should stay away from.

And Zach was that kind of man.

She didn't need him being a disruptive influence in her life—any more than she did in her class. She did her best to forget he was standing there and concentrated on Jessie instead.

"No, no, no," she scolded when the little girl chopped her way across the room in jerky little steps instead of slow, graceful ones. "Remember, you're a butterfly, fluttering over to sniff the flowers. Let me see you flutter."

"She's fluttering," came a voice behind her. "Give the kid a break."

Paige whirled around to face Zach. "She is *not* fluttering."

She saw a mixture of emotions in him, heat and ice, mingling in the silver-gray of his eyes. She whirled back around in a vain effort to ignore him. "Like this, Jessie." Feeling her limbs tremble uncharacteristically, she executed the step to show the child. "Now, you try it."

Jessie did, if a bit awkwardly.

"Looks like a flutter to me," came the voice behind them again, a voice that rumbled like bad weather.

She spun toward him, ready to send him to the moon, if it would get him out of her hair. "Why don't you go have a cup of coffee. The kitchen is at the top of the stairs and to the left. The coffee's hot."

He put up his hands. "Okay, okay, but if you need me—"

"I won't need you."

She wanted to spend the remaining twenty minutes of the class with Jessie—uninterrupted.

When he'd gone, she let out a sigh. "Is your daddy always like that?" she asked, sharing a small, woman-to-woman smile with Jessie.

Jessie giggled. "Sometimes. *Most* of the time."

Just as she'd thought. Paige rolled her eyes.

Zach found the coffeepot, then a cup with splashes of small red and blue flowers on it. He'd have preferred a man-size mug, but there were none in existence that he could see. In fact, everything in the kitchen was dainty and feminine from the print in the wallpaper to the row of tiny flowerpots sitting on the windowsill, soaking up the last of the day's early-spring sunshine.

From downstairs came Paige's voice calling out the ballet steps to Jessie in cadence and he frowned. He didn't like being away from the action, banished to the upstairs of the house.

He took a scalding swallow of black coffee. At least it wasn't milk toast-mild but strong and steamy, the way he liked it.

To entertain himself, he decided to check out the place. Through the arched doorway was a dining room with a cherrywood table and eight formal chairs. The set was old, probably a family heirloom, he decided. So was the small china cabinet and the dishes inside that looked too delicate to use.

He wondered if Paige held family gatherings here. Did she have a passel of brothers and sisters, parents, grandparents? He couldn't picture it. Somehow he thought of her as being alone and on her own.

A little uncertain of herself, but determined.

Beyond the dining room was the living room, empty of furniture except for a TV and a few fat toss pillows scattered on the floor in front of it. Bushy green plants vied for space at the windows, their leaves straining toward the light. Despite the lack of furniture, the room managed to look warm, inviting.

He glimpsed the single bedroom down the hall in colors of apricot and pale green and so feminine he could almost smell the scent of her perfume waft toward him. The whole house had a feminine appeal, as if Paige had consciously banished any semblance of the male perspective from it, as if she were somehow stating her independence. Or perhaps eradicating some man from her life.

That made him curious.

Who was Paige Hanford?

He took another swallow of coffee and reminded himself he shouldn't want to know, shouldn't care beyond the fact that she had talent and grace and had agreed to bring out some of both in Jessie.

He'd been adept at keeping women at arm's length, keeping the iron gate around his heart carefully locked, but he had the strong feeling that having any sort of relationship with a woman like Paige—small, feminine and so incredibly sexy—could put him at a definite risk.

Still, he was intrigued by her.

Definitely intrigued.

He'd just retraced his steps to the kitchen when he heard the sound of footsteps on the stairs.

Class was over.

Jessie bounded into the kitchen ahead of Paige. His daughter's cheeks were flushed, her dark, silken curls pulled into a ponytail at the side of her head like Paige's, a style she hadn't had when she'd arrived. Jessie had adopted an idol, or at least a role model, in her teacher.

"Thursday night I come for tap," she said, beaming. "Miss Paige is going to teach me all by myself. Like today."

"All by yourself, huh?" He gave Jessie a small smile, then swung his gaze to Paige. What the hell was wrong with his being included?

"That's right. No men allowed," Jessie chirped. "That's what Miss Paige said."

Well, he'd just see about that!

He didn't like being odd man out, not when it came to his own daughter. She was important to him. She was everything to him.

Still, he knew Jessie needed someone like Paige in her life. It was clear by the way she wanted to imitate her teacher that she worshiped her. Miss Paige had been all she'd talked about since that very first time they'd come here.

"I, uh, promised Jessie I'd take her for pizza after her lesson. Would you . . . care to join us?" He wasn't entirely sure why he was asking and, as soon as the words were out, began to regret them. Still, he found himself waiting for her answer.

"No, I couldn't. I . . ." Paige stopped, not knowing what excuse she could give. She just knew that she couldn't, *shouldn't* go. But it was tempting.

Very tempting.

She hadn't dated much since her divorce, though she supposed this wouldn't really be a date. It did, however, feel good to have a man want her company, even if it was only a friendly evening out for pizza.

Jessie was jumping up and down and saying, "Pretty please, pretty please" and Paige had to laugh.

She reconsidered. What could it hurt? "All right. If it's an early night."

If she stayed up until midnight, she could finish the typing she'd promised to have done by tomorrow, she calculated. This odd job brought in the much-needed money to get her studio off to a successful start and to put funds in the coffers for the recital.

She'd taken on a lot by trying to have a recital the first year, but it was important to the students, as well as the future of her school.

"I promise to have you home by Jessie's bedtime. That early enough?" Zach asked.

She thought she saw a hint of a smile, a real smile, on his sexy mouth.

"I'll need to change first." She glanced down at her dance wear, then back up at him. He was eyeing it, too—and not drawing the same conclusion she was.

Paige swallowed nervously and remembered—belatedly—this was not a man she should get involved with.

"No problem," he said. "Jessie and I will swing by for you in, say... an hour?"

"Fine."

He gathered up Jessie's dance bag and went out the door, asking Jessie how her lesson had gone and thinking about the sexy Miss Paige.

Chapter Three

Libertydale had two pizza places, one for the grab-a-quick-slice crowd and the other where people dawdled and made an evening of it. It also had playtime enticements for the children.

Fun House Pizzeria was full of kids swarming over the bright play equipment, which made the evening seem nothing like a date.

Until she glanced at Zach, looking seductive and gorgeous across from her. Then her stomach clenched, her palms grew sweaty and her heart did a little tap dance in her chest—all the things that happen on a first date.

No—she wouldn't think of it as that. Zach saw her as someone who could teach dance to his daughter and maybe instill a little feminine grace in the child along the way. This was just an outing, a friendly sharing of pizza.

Then why did his silver-eyed gaze settle on her mouth as if he wanted to taste it? Why did that gaze slide over every inch of her as if he were hungry—and not for pizza? She squirmed in her chair, then picked up her napkin and spread it across her lap, wishing the blue-and-white checked square was big enough to hide behind.

Lifting her chin a determined notch, she smiled across the table at him. "Have you lived in Liberty-dale long?" she asked, deciding to get the evening onto a conversational footing.

"Jessie and I moved here about a year ago." His gaze strayed across the room to where his daughter climbed on the back of a bright green turtle. He'd kept a cautious eye on her ever since she'd left the table for the play area, watching her almost obsessively.

What was he afraid of? That she would fall, skin a knee?

Seemingly satisfied she was all right, he turned back to Paige. "There was an opening in the D.A.'s office then and I decided to take it."

"And do you like it here?" A year ago was when Jessie's mother died, she remembered.

He nodded. "It's a safe town, quiet, secure." His gaze returned to Jessie for a brief moment.

A strange choice of words to describe the town. Most people used terms like picturesque, small, mid-dle-American. Zach called it safe.

It was that, of course—she just wondered why it had been the first thing to come to mind.

"Where was home?" she asked.

"Home?" A flicker of something—pain?—crossed his face. "Chicago."

He might have said more but just then the waiter interrupted to inform them they were all out of the peppers Zach had ordered on his pizza. He substituted black olives instead.

"Enough about me," he said when the waiter left. "Tell me about Paige."

What about Paige? A few years ago she would have said there wasn't much to tell. But that was before she'd begun to rebuild her life, recover her independence. She smiled. "I was lucky enough to grow up here. When I was Jessie's age, I danced in my first recital on the stage in the old Majestic Theater. I was a flower—a buttercup."

A grin stole across his face as if he could imagine it. "And you were wonderful."

She felt light, reckless. And smug about herself. "Of course I was wonderful."

They both laughed, and she decided she liked the sound Zach Delano made when he was amused. She wanted to amuse him more—so she could hear it again. So he would keep looking at her the way he was now—as if she were the most important woman in the place.

Laugh lines crinkled at the corners of his eyes, the edges of his mouth. His teeth were white and even in his tanned, square face and his eyes danced with delight. For a brief while, he even forgot to glance at Jessie with that watchful scan.

"I grew up in a tough Chicago neighborhood. A town like Libertydale would have seemed like heaven." His fingers caught the tips of hers ever so lightly. "Tell me what you did as a kid."

Paige could barely breathe, could barely think, she was so conscious of the heat passing between their fingertips. She tried to remember the warm summer days, the snowy school holidays. She wanted to tell him everything, share it all with him.

"We did the usual, caught lightning bugs in the summer, capturing them in washed pickle jars with holes punched in the lid, we staged a pet parade down Main Street to the park every fall. Billy Sowers always won—he had a ten-foot python that he loved to scare the girls with."

"Bill Sowers who runs the Stop-N-Shop?"

"One and the same."

"And what pet did you have?"

"A collie that someone had dumped at the side of the highway. I begged my father to let me keep him. Beau rode in my doll buggy when he was a puppy, then later I dressed him in a pink tulle tutu. He hated those parades. The next year he hid under the porch and wouldn't come out."

"That's the kind of life I want for Jessie." He grew solemn.

"What is it, Zach? What are you trying to protect her from?"

"Everything."

She'd barely heard his one-word answer. It hadn't been meant as a prelude to a conversation but as the end to one. If she expected to learn more about Zach, she'd been mistaken. Then his eyes smiled.

"So, you outgrew pet parades and dance recitals in the old Majestic, then what? Went off to New York to seek your fame and fortune?"

"No." Now Paige knew what it was like to be asked the personal. She wanted to clam up the way he had. Or at least change the subject, but Zach apparently had more practice at it than she had. She took a slow sip of her cola, then answered, absently pleating her napkin between her fingers. "I gave up dancing and got married instead, thinking it was what I wanted. It . . . it wasn't a good marriage. I ended it a year and a half ago, moved back here and started Dance-Works."

"And Jessie and I are glad that you did."

He meant it. She could tell by the shimmer of warmth in his eyes and the soft smile that crept onto his lips.

His lips. They were garnering far more of her attention than they should. But she couldn't help thinking what it would be like to kiss him. She squeezed her eyes shut, willing the thought to pass.

"So how did she do?"

Paige glanced up. "Pardon?" He had her at a loss. That's what she got for thinking about kisses instead of conversation. She'd been enjoying the evening, enjoying Zach—and the way he made her feel.

"Jessie...how did she do in class today? Your professional opinion."

"Oh." She traced a droplet of moisture down the side of her glass. He'd asked and she owed him an honest answer, she knew. "I think she did very well. Jessie has a lot of heart—and I admire that."

"She loves to dance. Thank you for giving her that chance."

Paige toyed with her straw, feeling the heat of his gaze on her. She only hoped she wasn't complicating her life. "We'll take it one lesson at a time," she said. "I'll see how she does."

Just then, Jessie bounded over to the table, ending their discussion.

"You through playing, sugar?" Zach gave her ponytail a playful tug.

"I got hungry, Daddy."

"Come on, then, let's go see if that pizza's ready." He excused himself to Paige, and the pair walked toward the counter, Jessie chattering like a magpie.

Paige watched as father and daughter conversed, Zach seemingly entranced by Jessie's every word. She looked like a tiny doll, marching along beside his towering strength, small and cherished and loved.

And protected—overly protected.

He might just be trying too hard to be both father and mother to Jessie. But Paige suspected it was more than that.

Zach Delano was a man who was used to being in command—whether it was in the courtroom or in his daughter's life.

Paige had had her fill of domineering men, men who hovered and stole a woman's independence. If she were wise, she'd listen to her instincts that were clanging in her brain, warning her against getting any more involved with Zach than she already was.

That would be a whole lot easier, she thought, if the man didn't affect her like a bolt of lightning every time she looked at him.

Zach turned around, the tray of pizza in his hands, and caught Paige frowning into her straw with a vehemence he couldn't fathom. What, he wondered, had prompted it? And why was he having such a difficult time curbing this fascination with her?

She looked so achingly tempting in her oversize pink sweater and those soft-washed jeans that fit just tight enough to render a man helpless.

The woman was too soft and feminine to be considered safe territory. He should have realized that before inviting her into his life.

They would share a pizza, then he'd take her home, he vowed silently. And he'd keep hands off. No goodnight kiss on her doorstep, not even a casual peck on the end of that pert, uptilted nose of hers.

She glanced up as he neared the table, her eyes wide and shimmery green under the overhead lighting. A few wispy ends of her tawny hair escaped her ponytail and teased around her face. Her lips parted slightly for a moment, then curved upward into a faint smile—a shaky smile. Hell, she was as nervous about this evening as he was, he realized.

Why? Did he affect her as much as she was affecting him? God help her, if that was the case. He trembled inside just looking at her, the soft brush of their fingertips earlier had nearly set him on fire.

Yes, he was definitely going to have to keep his hands off when he took her home.

"Mmm, that smells delicious," Paige said as Zach slid the piping-hot pizza in front of her. "What do you think, Jessie?"

Jessie had just slid into the chair next to Paige. "I think this place makes the best pizza in the whoooole world," she said, one little leg pumping up and down frenetically.

"You do, huh?" Zach smiled over at her. "Then I guess I can't have your share."

"Nuh-uh."

The pizza was indeed good, Paige thought, taking a bite. Maybe even the best in the world as Jessie proclaimed. They all ate hungrily for a while, too busy for conversation beyond an occasional murmur of ecstasy over the tasty treat.

"I hafta go to the bathroom, Daddy," Jessie announced halfway through her second slice. A dab of pizza sauce clung to her small chin.

"Okay, honey." Zach put down his napkin and scraped back his chair.

"I can take her," Paige offered.

"Yes, Paige can take me." Jessie wore a smile, as if this were a great honor, and scooted energetically off her seat.

"You don't mind?" Zach gave Paige a questioning glance.

"Not at all. Just don't eat all the pizza while we're gone," she returned, then reached out for Jessie's eager hand.

She wondered how Zach handled situations such as this one. Somehow, she couldn't picture the big, sexy man loitering outside ladies' rooms, trying to explain his presence there to curious female onlookers. A man trying to raise a daughter alone had to meet with difficult obstacles at times, something she'd only begun to realize.

Jessie hopped and skipped ahead of her. Paige wondered if she missed not having a mother like other children had. A wave of tenderness swept over her for the brave little girl.

"My daddy said I'm special," Jessie announced on the way. "He said that's why you wanted to teach me all by myself."

Paige had to smile. Was there anything Zach didn't think of when it came to protecting his little darling? It seemed not.

"I thought it would be nice if we worked together for a while," she said, realizing she didn't want the child hurt any more than Jessie's father did. "Do you mind taking class alone?"

Jessie cocked her head to one side, as if thinking through her answer for a moment. "No. It's fun."

"That's good."

Jessie managed to take care of her bathroom chore all by herself, then allowed Paige to turn on the faucet and dispense the pretty pink soap her hands couldn't reach. They shared the electric hand dryer, and Paige fixed the satin bow on Jessie's ponytail.

"I like to wear my hair like yours," Jessie said, peering up at Paige through her pink frames, slightly crooked on her little nose.

Paige smiled and adjusted them, feeling a second pang of tenderness for the motherless little girl.

Zach was waiting for them when they returned. He hadn't eaten any more than his fair share of the pizza, and now leaned back in his chair, rubbing his stomach, obviously replete. Jessie declared herself full, too, after another three bites. Paige tried to eat more but was all too aware of Zach's heated gaze on her, and soon put down the slice she'd been nibbling. Zach was giving her butterflies. Big-time.

"Can we wrap up the rest and take it home to Mr. Murphy?" Jessie pleaded with her father.

"Mr. Murphy's her dog," Zach explained at Paige's questioning look. "And the last time we took him pizza, he kept us awake all night baying at the moon with major indigestion."

Paige had to laugh.

"I don't think so, Jessie. You can feed him a few kibbles, and he'll thank you for it."

Jessie didn't look convinced.

"Now, we'd better get you home before Ernestine has my hide."

Zach dropped a tip on the table, and they headed for the door.

"Do you mind if I take Jessie home first?" he asked Paige. "Ernestine is serious about bedtimes and it's on the way."

"Of course not." Paige would have preferred having Jessie as a buffer between them, as she'd been for the first part of the evening, but she knew it was late and Jessie had had a big day.

It was a short drive to Zach's house, a rambling two story with a nice lawn and a big wraparound porch. Ernestine met them at the door, arms folded across her chest, one orthopedic tennis shoe tapping in dictatorial displeasure.

Paige had the idea that she was about to come face-to-face with the only female who could outdominate Zach. And this she was eager to see.

"Not only did you feed her pizza again, but you kept my baby out till all hours," the autocrat boomed

from the doorway. Zach had described her as a battleship—and the term was apt.

But Zach remained undaunted by her lack of
charm, chucking the woman lightly under the chin and
offering her his biggest beguiling smile. "Now, Ernie,
you know how she loves the stuff. And I'm sorry
about the time. It sorta got away from us."

The woman only harrumphed, but Paige could de-
tect a softening. She would do well to remember this
little incident in future dealings with the man before
she found herself succumbing as easily as Ernestine.

"Ernestine, this is Miss Paige Hanford," Zach said
when the housekeeper deigned to move her goodly
frame out of the doorway so they could step into the
tiled entry hall.

Jessie had spied Mr. Murphy and raced off to explain to the brown-and-white ball of fur that he had to
eat kibbles tonight. Paige wasn't certain what kind of
dog he was, probably just a lovable mutt.

"Hello, Ernestine," Paige said, adding a warm
smile for the woman who was blatantly eyeing her up
and down. The housekeeper obviously didn't consider her perusal rude, but Paige was beginning to feel
oddly uncomfortable.

"There's not much to you, is there, child?" she said
as if Paige were ten and had a lot of growing to do yet.

"There's enough, Ernie," Zach said, adding his
own brand of perusal and raising Paige's already
soaring body temperature a few sultry degrees.

"Jessie seems to like you. Miss Paige is all I hear about from morning till night," Ernestine said with another *harrumph*.

"I'm going to run Paige home now," Zach interjected. "Tell Jessie I'll be back to tuck her in."

"As if *I* couldn't do it," the housekeeper muttered. She gave him a sharp scowl, then added, "You just plain spoil that girl. There's no other word for it."

They said their goodbyes and headed out the door. "She's not very friendly, is she?" Paige commented when they were safely out of earshot.

"Ernie? This was one of her mellower days."

Paige laughed. "I'd sure hate to be around when she was in a *real* snit."

"I know. She's a tyrant, but she loves Jessie. And she tolerates me."

Paige raised a disbelieving eyebrow. "Tolerates? Don't give me that! Your charm had the woman's garters popping."

"Well... let's say I know my way around her."

Paige would bet he knew his way around a lot of women, but she didn't intend to become one of them. Then she rethought that. She already had. Hadn't he neatly sweet-talked her into putting Jessie back into dance class? When Zach opened the car door for her, she climbed into the four-by-four and settled into the seat, feeling wishy-washy indeed.

Paige knew this neighborhood. It was one of the more established in the town, with well-built older homes and full, leafy trees that formed a shady canopy over the street in midsummer. Old-fashioned street lamps dispelled the dark spring night and cast cozy shadows over everything. Her own neighborhood was just as nice, though the homes had been built on a smaller scale. But her compact bungalow afforded all the room she needed.

The street lamp illuminated Zach's profile as he maneuvered past parked cars and finally onto Missouri Avenue, one of the east-west thoroughfares that would take them to her house.

"I enjoyed tonight," she said, meaning it. "I'm glad you and Jessie invited me along."

He turned and glanced over at her. "I had a good time, too." His voice was a low, lazy drawl. And sexy—definitely sexy. His gaze lingered for a moment too long on her lips, then his own curved upward in a slightly crooked smile.

Paige swallowed hard and looked away. The man was far too handsome for her peace of mind. And with her remark, she'd probably just sent him a dangerously mixed message.

This evening had somehow seemed more innocent when Jessie was along. Paige hadn't had many dates since her divorce. In the experience department she was a total babe-in-the-woods. And one who found the man she was with very attractive.

"There's my street," she said, more for something to say than anything else.

He smiled again. "I see it."

He wheeled the four-by-four onto Larkspur Lane and, five houses down, turned into her driveway.

"Well, I'll let you get back so you can tuck Jessie in," she said as she reached for the door handle.

"I'm sure Ernestine has it all under control." He killed the engine and came around to her side.

Of course, she thought.

She climbed out of the Bronco—an ungainly exit from a vehicle more suited to men of Zach's stature than to women of hers—and slid into Zach's receptive arms. Her hands flattened against the soft fleece of his sweater, her senses all too aware of the hard muscles beneath it. The warmth of his breath stirred against her hair.

He smelled like the freshness of the spring night, with all the promise of something to come. Something wonderful or something dangerous, the aura he exuded could be either. Or both.

All she knew at that moment was that she wanted to find out.

Chapter Four

Zach had just meant to offer Paige some help out of the Bronco, but suddenly feeling her in his arms, her soft, feminine scent teasing him, the moonlight glinting off the full pout of her lips, he knew he had to kiss her.

Just once.

He lowered his mouth to hers, but with the first brush of her lips, the first glory of her pliant temptation, he was lost. Paige was splendor and heat and wanton passion, all in one tiny dynamite package.

Her hands traveled up from his chest and wound softly around his neck. He drew her to him, her small, rounded breasts pressed enticingly against him. Desire, swift and undeniable, leaped from some dark part of him, a part he thought he'd buried deep in his soul.

But Paige, soft and tender and inviting, had brought him back to that dangerous precipice of feelings, the edge he'd vowed he'd never get close to again.

Her mouth was sorcery, tasting of wanton sweetness. He groaned in need—and in regret that he had no power to pull away. He wanted more of her, the risk he ran forgotten in the heat of her.

Paige had expected the kiss would be dangerous, but she hadn't bargained for this wild rush of feeling. Her heart thudded, her pulse quickened and her hormones went totally berserk. Zach tasted like the danger of the night and the heat of a thousand fires.

His mouth moved over hers in sensual slowness, then demanding need. Though some still-sentient part of her brain shouted in warning, her body ignored it. She crushed her hips against him and felt him harden in response, heard a ragged moan from low in his throat. Of pleasure? Or the same sweet torture that tore through her?

His tongue teased at her lips, begging them to part, and when she opened to him, he awakened her to a whole new round of feelings. Heat coiled low in her body as his tongue danced with hers. They tasted each other, seeking each other's sweet secrets.

Desire swamped her senses, overwhelming her, but in the distance, reality shimmered, hazy, fuzzy, but present—and eventually it won out.

"Zach . . ."

She drew away, just an inch, but enough for good
sense to return.

He stroked her cheek. "I shouldn't have done that,"
he murmured. "I invited you for pizza, not for a
quick—I mean—"

"I know." Paige understood his words. This was
just a casual outing, but the kiss made it something
more, much more. "Zach...if I'm going to work with
Jessie, we...we shouldn't complicate things."

"That may not be as easy as you think." He traced
her lower lip with the tip of his finger, the touch nearly
more than she could bear. "Come on," he said, "I'll
walk you to your door."

"No. The porch light is on. I'll be fine." Before he
could argue with that, she turned toward the house.
Front doors and porch steps had a way of inviting one
last good-night kiss, and she was still reeling from the
first one. As if she'd been shot out of a cannon, in
fact.

Reaching the porch, she turned and waved to Zach,
then twisted the key in the lock and escaped inside.

Zach watched until Paige had closed the door and
flipped on a few lights. Her faint shadow teased at him
through the gauzy front drape for a moment, soft,
small and alluring, then it disappeared from view.

The all-too-tempting Paige had rocked him back on
his heels, but good. His lips still sang with the taste of
her, his body marked with the imprint of her soft
curves. He'd vowed to keep his hands off, not just

Paige, but any woman who posed even the slightest threat of serious involvement.

He'd forgotten that vow.

With a silent curse he rounded the Bronco and climbed in behind the wheel. He sat there for a moment, staring out into the night, and waited for reality to return, waiting for the past to seep back into his memory and remind him of a few painful facts, mainly that life wasn't as simple as an evening out with Paige for pizza.

Life carried a threat. He had only to think of Janet and the horror of the rainy night that had taken her from Jessie and him, the devastating night that had shattered his delusion that harm could be kept at bay.

The three of them had been so smug in their happy little world. He'd believed safe and secure were a given, but he didn't anymore.

He'd blamed himself every night since. If only he'd driven Janet to her parents' house himself. If he'd been the one behind the wheel, he might have seen that drunk driver coming, might have been able to swerve out of the way. But it had been Janet driving, Janet who'd swerved too late. And it had cost her her life.

No, life wasn't simple. It was complicated.

And sometimes cruel.

Shoving the Bronco into reverse, he backed out of the driveway and started toward home.

He'd promised to tuck Jessie in.

It was five o'clock and Zach had a mountain of work to finish. His desk resembled a paper factory hit by a tornado. He still had to meet with an investigator on the case he was trying next week—and Jessie had a dance lesson with Paige tonight.

He cast a quick glance at the wall clock with the bent hour hand, then back at the mushrooming pile of papers in front of him.

Sinking back in his desk chair, he dialed home.

Ernestine answered on the fifth ring. "Ah, my favorite girl," he purred into the receiver. "Ernie, I need a favor."

"You always do when you start a conversation like that. I'm not a slice short of a twelve-inch pizza, you know, so this better be good."

"Ernie, I'm nothing if not good."

He heard her doubtful snort. "You want me to take Jessie to her dance lesson, am I right?"

"Please. You don't have to wait for her—in fact, Paige is against it—just be there to pick her up again an hour later. The lesson starts at seven. I promise to be home by nine. Oh, and Ernie, make sure Jessie wears her glasses."

"You're the one who gives in to her on that one— not me," she barked into the phone.

"I know, I know. Talk to you later, Ernie." He hung up before the woman could launch into a few other complaints about his laxness when it came to disciplining his daughter. So what if he spared the rod a little where Jessie was concerned? What did it hurt?

He knew she didn't always wear her glasses as she should, knew some of the kids in the neighborhood teased her, called her four eyes, knew Jessie felt odd, different when she wore them.

He didn't want Jessie to feel different from other children. He wanted her life to be as normal as possible—but it wasn't. Her life, *their* life, had come apart in the space of one night—and Zach didn't know how to put it back together for her again.

Jessie had been left shaken, uncertain—uncertain of herself, of her world, a world devoid of a mother to tuck her in, to pin a bow in her hair, to tell her she was pretty.

Zach had tried to soften her pain in every way he knew how. He protected her, spoiled her, but Jessie hadn't responded—until lately. Until dance class.

And Paige.

Paige had been his first ray of hope for his daughter. She'd been the first woman Jessie had reached out to, except—on some level—to Ernestine.

Ernestine was wonderful, an excellent housekeeper and all-around majordomo. He relied on her for everything, but Jessie needed more than what Ernestine, alone, could offer.

Short of his taking a wife, a new mother for Jessie, which he wasn't ready to do, Paige had come along at just the right moment.

There was only one problem.

He was too damned attracted to her.

He could still taste the sweet lushness of her lips. Her face splashed into his memory far too often while he'd worked the past few days.

Maybe it was better that Ernestine was taking Jessie to class tonight instead of himself. He needed a little more distance from Paige Hanford, a little more time to forget the way the moonlight could tip her lashes silver, sheen her lips a pearly pink.

Kissable pink.

He groaned and dragged both hands through his hair until his fingers nearly grooved his scalp. Paige occupied too much of his mind, held his thoughts hostage. He couldn't quit thinking about her.

And Jessie couldn't quit talking about her.

He knew his daughter would be disappointed he wasn't taking her to class himself, but he couldn't risk seeing Paige again.

Not until he was more in control.

Paige stacked the last of the pages she'd been typing beside the word processor. Later tonight, after Jessie's lesson, she would scan them for accuracy. She needed this job, needed every penny of money the extra typing brought in. For DanceWorks. It hadn't been easy starting her own school, but she'd done it. And she was proud of her achievement.

Stephen had said she'd fail. He'd filled her with doubts all through their four-year marriage. In an effort—she realized now—to keep her tied to him.

He'd laughed when she'd told him she was leaving, that she was going back home to start over again, that she no longer loved him. He'd said she couldn't make it on her own; that she needed him, his protection, the life he'd provided her with.

There had been times, scary times, when she'd almost believed him—but not quite. She'd come home, determined to make it, determined to prove to the world, to herself—and maybe even to Stephen—that she could do it.

DanceWorks was now a reality, a shaky reality, but her own personal accomplishment. The recital would soon be another reality.

She only had to keep her focus—that meant not allowing Zach Delano to derail her thoughts, sidetrack her from her sense of purpose. She wasn't sure that would be an easy task, considering that she'd be seeing the man each time Jessie came for her lesson.

Jessie.

Paige glanced at her watch. The girl would be here any moment now. Jessie and Zach. She touched a hand to her hair to check for flying loose ends and to make sure that the pale green ribbon she'd carefully threaded through her long braid this morning was in place.

Just then she heard the doorbell to her studio. She ran a hand down her black leotard, the one that fit her glove snug. Flipping off her word processor, she headed for the door.

Jessie stood on the stoop, clutching her dance bag in her hands. The color of her tights and leotard matched her glasses, which she was wearing tonight. Ernestine flanked her like a mother pachyderm.

Paige hid her wash of disappointment that it was Ernestine, not Zach, who'd come with Jessie.

"We're early," the woman announced, "but the child just couldn't sit still another minute. Kept asking if it was time to leave yet, so I hope it's okay."

"Of course. It's fine, Ernie." Paige smiled at Jessie. "I'm glad you're ready to get started. Come on in." She held the door open for her pupil.

"I'll be back for her at eight," Ernestine said. "Mr. Delano said I didn't need to wait."

Right, Paige thought, only Zach waited. And watched her every move, making her blood heat in her veins and a shiver run up her spine.

"See you later, Ernestine," she said as the woman turned to leave.

Again she hid her disappointment that Jessie had arrived without her hunk daddy in tow. Why hadn't he brought Jessie to class? Was he trying to avoid her and the devastation of the kiss they'd shared the other night, the lightning-shock reaction they seemed to have toward each other?

Paige was still trying to forget its impact.

Jessie had clattered down the stairs to the studio ahead of her and now sat on the piano bench, attempting to tie the black ribbon on her tap shoe.

"Let me help you with that, Jessie," she said when she realized Jessie had knotted it hopelessly.

"I got it in a tangle," she said as she stuck her shoe out for Paige, black ribbons dangling.

Paige worked at the knot, trying to loosen it. She remembered how she'd tangled her own laces the night of her first recital and how her mother had been there to help her, calming her jittery young fingers.

Her mother had worked behind the scenes, playing stage-mom, finding lost shoes, calming nerves, assuring little dancers that missing sequins wouldn't be noticed by anyone in the audience.

Paige couldn't remember a time when her mother hadn't been there for her. She had moved to Arizona five years ago, shortly after Paige's father had died, but Paige always knew her mother was just a phone call away.

Jessie only had Zach. Maybe the girl needed her—just a little. As good as that made her feel, it was also a little scary. The more involved she became with Jessie, the more involved she'd be with Zach.

And given the way the man affected her, that could be dangerous.

"There...all tied," she said when she'd finished securing the bow so Jessie wouldn't trip over it, a very real possibility.

"Thanks, Miss Paige." With a smile, the child scooted off the bench. "Ernestine says I hafta wear my glasses tonight." Her smile faded a little.

Paige knelt down on one knee so she'd be eye level with her young charge. "Is that so bad, Jessie? They look very pretty on you. You should wear them all the time."

Jessie gave her a grave look. "But dancers don't wear glasses."

"Some do." Paige wasn't sure it was a fact, but Jessie needed to believe it.

"They do?" Her expression brightened.

"Well, of course." Paige tugged the girl's ponytail. "How else will they be able to see if their audience is smiling?"

Jessie gave this a moment of thought.

"There's no reason you can't be the best dancer out there, as pretty as any dancer on the stage," Paige told her.

Jessie smiled at that.

"Now...I think we'd better get started or Ernestine will be back to get you...and we won't be through with our class."

Jessie giggled and pushed her glasses up on her nose.

The lesson went well. But Jessie's improved vision didn't translate into improved talent. At least not discernibly. But Paige would give it time...Jessie was a little uncertain of life, uncertain of her own worth— and that was something Paige could understand.

She'd had her own self-worth challenged during the years of her marriage. But she'd found her own feet. And she wanted Jessie to do the same.

Ernestine was back in an hour as she'd promised. "How did the child do?" she asked.

Zach would no doubt demand a full accounting of the class, and Ernestine intended to be prepared, Paige thought with a smile.

"It was a good lesson," she said in all honesty. "Jessie has some steps she's going to practice at home."

"On my fresh-polished kitchen floor, most likely," Ernestine said haughtily. But Paige was sure it was all an act to hide the fact that she adored Jessie as much as Zach did.

Paige longed to ask the woman more about Zach, why he seemed so protective of little Jessie. But just then, the child clambered up the stairs from the studio, where she'd been changing out of her dance shoes, and the opportunity was lost.

And Zach's life, the reasons he protected Jessie so guardedly, were really none of her business, she reminded herself sharply.

As Paige said good-night to Jessie, the girl reached up and gave her a hesitant hug around the neck. Paige was sure she'd never felt anything as sweet.

It was a balmy day for early spring, and Paige had a garageful of scenery props to build if she expected to have them ready in time for the recital. The dusty old theater she'd rented for her little production didn't come equipped with backdrops, so Paige had to improvise.

The day was warm enough to work with the garage door open. She'd donned an old, stretched-out sweatshirt and a pair of threadbare jeans she'd found in the back of the closet, gathered a hammer, nails and a huge supply of plywood sufficient enough to build a soccer stadium and then set to work.

It was the first Saturday afternoon she'd had without lessons scheduled, perfect for getting started on this necessary project.

Over the past few days, she'd been busy with classes, not to mention making hard decisions about which of her little charmers would have solo numbers in the recital, mainly the more advanced of her troupe. She'd hung a giant Recital Checklist on her dining-room wall, but so far, few things had been marked completed.

She still had costumes to design, a seamstress yet to find, a myriad of duties that had kept her mind occupied, too occupied to give Zach Delano more than a passing thought.

She hadn't heard from him—not that she'd expected to—but he was always there, at the edges of her mind. At night he paraded into her dreams uninvited, along with the memory of the kiss they'd shared in the moonlight, a kiss she had no business remembering with such clarity.

Paige fitted a board to a precut piece of plywood to act as a base—the wooden stand jutting out the backside of the prop so dancing feet didn't trip on it—and hammered in a nail. After doing the same to the other end, she stood the prop upright.

With a little paint, it would become a New York City skyline. A perfect backdrop for the Top-Hat-and-Tails tap number, she thought, cocking her head to one side to picture it finished, her students soft-shoeing their way across the stage in front of it.

"Isn't that board a little jagged?" a male voice behind her said.

Paige whirled around to find Zach standing in her garage, studying her handiwork. "It's the New York skyline—or at least it will be with a little spray paint," she added.

What was he doing here? This wasn't the day for Jessie's lesson. And Jessie wasn't with him. He was alone. Alone and looking too gorgeous for words.

He gave the prop a scrutinizing glance. One eyebrow raised quizzically, as if he were trying to understand the purpose of an abstract sculpture in the park that would better serve as a perch for birds than a work of art. "I haven't been to New York in a long time," he said wryly. "Maybe it's changed."

"Thanks a whole lot for your vote of confidence in my artistic ability." Paige clamped three nails between her teeth and picked up the hammer again, ready to tackle the next precut board.

The man at the lumberyard hadn't been this critical when she'd shown him the patterns of what she'd wanted cut. She pounded a block of wood to the back of this prop, a row of dancing flowers she intended to paint in colors of red, blue and green.

"Did you come to find out how Jessie's doing with her lessons? I'd have thought Ernestine had filled you in. Or Jessie." She didn't glance up. It was better to keep her eyes on the plywood rather than his quirky smile or the heat in his eyes when his gaze settled on her face or the way his crisp white shirt hugged his torso and his faded jeans sheathed his powerful legs.

"Jessie did—all about it." Endlessly, Zach thought. His daughter had hardly left out a detail. And what she had left out, his overheated imagination readily supplied—Paige's lithe body moving in rhythm, the swing of her long tawny braid above her delectable derriere, her smile that made her face glow as soft and intimate as candlelight.

"And did she tell you I'm pleased with her progress?"

"She did." He smiled. "She's been practicing hard. In fact, that's what I came to talk to you about."

"Oh?"

He moved closer to where she worked. Her undeniable fragrance curled around him, so smolderingly sensual in its allure that it made him doubt his wisdom in coming here. He'd told himself he'd come for a purpose, but now he suspected that purpose was more an excuse to see Paige again.

She'd turned her face up to his, giving him all her attention, and Zach wasn't sure he could handle it. He shoved his hands into his pockets and paced across the small, single-car garage she was using as a workshop.

It wasn't safe being this close to her.

"Jessie's been trying out her new ballet steps in Ernestine's kitchen, using the chair backs for a...a..."

"A *barre,*" she supplied.

"Yeah. A *barre.*"

She smiled. "I used a few kitchen chairs when I was that age. And bathroom towel racks were definitely on the endangered list in our house. I pulled more than one of them out of the wall."

Zach grinned. He could picture a young Paige learning her craft. He wondered if she'd had summertime freckles or knobby knees. His gaze skimmed over her appreciatively. There wasn't a knobby bone in her body now. She was filled out in all the right places.

"I want to install a *barre* at home for Jessie," he said. "Maybe put in a mirrored wall behind it, like the one in your studio."

He saw her eyes widen in surprise, then soften to a wistful green. "Jessie's a very special little girl," she said quietly.

"Yeah, well, I want to do it for her. But I need your help."

"Oh?"

"Yes. To show me how high to place it."

"I see."

"I know you're busy." He waved a hand at her project. "Maybe I could, uh, finish up this little job for you in return. In fact, it should be a piece of cake."

He gave her work area a cursory glance. An unfinished prop stood in the middle of it. Bits of wood lay scattered about, along with various-size nails and an array of tools he wondered if she knew how to use with any adroitness.

But at the moment she didn't look at all eager to accept his help. Her chin had raised to a rather obdurate angle and she was regarding him warily.

"What's the matter? Don't you trust me with a hammer?"

Paige didn't trust him not to take over. Men somehow always became superior when they had a hammer in their hand. "Thank you, but I think I can handle this 'piece of cake' on my own." Maybe she was overreacting, but this was her project—not the *little job* he considered it.

Zach shrugged, realizing he'd miffed her somehow. "Sorry, just thought you might want some help."

"I don't." She turned back to her work and hammered in a nail sharply. "As for the *barre* for Jessie, I suppose I could give you some advice on installing it. But deciding on the height isn't all that difficult."

Yes, he'd definitely miffed her. But why, he wasn't sure. He watched her work, a few nails clamped between her pretty teeth. She seemed to know what she wanted to do, but she was going about it all wrong, he decided.

"I, uh, think you could use a little of my expertise," he said finally. He grinned as her head came up and her chin lifted to an even more precipitous angle than before. Then he went into territory where most any fool would fear to tread. "That nail's entirely too short for that thickness of board."

When she didn't throw the hammer at his head, he knelt down beside her and her project. "I assume you're attempting to make a base for this, but it would stand much more sturdily if you widened the space between the feet. Set them out here at the ends to give the prop more stability."

Paige wanted to curse. She didn't remember asking for his help, but he'd just rolled up his sleeves as if he owned the place, scavenging around in the old box of miscellaneous nails she'd found up in the rafters of the garage, nails left by the former residents of the house.

So maybe some of her supplies weren't the best. Her budget for this recital was shoestring, and she was grateful for any trip she didn't have to make to the hardware store.

"Look, these short nails do the trick. See that prop over there." She indicated the one she'd finished a short time before. *On her own.* "It's standing quite nicely. Without any help from you, I might add."

He dropped the nails that he had in his hand and glanced at the standing prop. "Hmm," he said, then got to his feet and sauntered over to it. With a tap of his finger, it began to wobble. He tapped it harder and it toppled over, landing on the ancient lawnmower she'd found in a garage sale last fall.

"Well, sure," she said. "Just shove it over."

He gave her a disarming male grin. "Doesn't look like it would have stood up to a light sneeze to me."

"I don't recall asking you."

His grin widened at that. "Maybe... But the fact remains, you could use my help."

Paige tried to tell herself this man wasn't Stephen. He wasn't laughing at her and telling her she'd fail at anything she tried. But he *was* telling her she needed him. And that struck too close to a raw nerve in her.

"Look, Zach, I can do this on my own."

"Sure—but think how much faster it will go if we do it together."

"Together..."

Chapter Five

Paige suspected she'd be sorry. She usually was when she didn't listen to her own inner reasoning. She wasn't entirely sure why she'd weakened and allowed him to help her with the props, maybe because they were cumbersome, maybe because he was entirely too persuasive, maybe because he'd used the word *together*—which implied sharing equally.

And maybe she was just a sucker for ruggedly appealing men. Stephen had seemed ruggedly appealing—in the beginning, she thought with increased wariness.

But whatever her reasons, she'd agreed to accept Zach's help and now she needed to have the good grace to welcome it.

"Two props down, eight more to go," he said, reaching for another precut piece of plywood. "Who'd you buy these sheets from? I hope not Wilburton's Lumberyard."

"What's wrong with Wilburton's?" she asked, feeling herself tense inside. Larry Wilburton had sold them to her himself and had one of his yardmen cut them to her specifications.

"They charge an arm and a leg. Old Soak-em Larry just lies in wait for any chump who happens into his lair. Hand me one of those long nails over there," he said, motioning to her right.

Gritting her teeth, she did.

"So where did you get this stuff?" He picked up the hammer and drove the nail into the board cleanly.

Paige knew she could lie—but lying had never been something she was all that comfortable with. "From Soak-em Larry, if you must know."

He flashed her a quick, disappointed smile.

"He gave me a deal. He happens to have a niece in one of my classes."

"A deal? Larry wouldn't give his own aged grandmother a deal."

This "togetherness" wasn't going at all well.

"What difference does it make where the plywood came from? It's my plywood now."

He glanced up. "I just don't like to see anyone get taken in, that's all."

If she'd been taken in, it was by this man wielding a hammer in her garage, promising help, then offering criticism she didn't want or need.

"Look, just pound. How wide I loosen my purse strings is my business." She hammered in another nail—a *short* one, in defiance. It made her feel better. Then she tested the block of wood. It held.

Maybe it was a man thing, the belief that carpentry was a male-only province, that women were somehow lacking the gene necessary to grasp the concept, the same gene that enabled them to understand car repair.

And football.

With that conclusion arrived at, she stood the finished prop upright and admired the result. An excitement rippled through her, as it did whenever she imagined opening night. Her debut production...the stage ablaze with lights...the music...the dancers...

Zach hadn't offered any further comments, for which she was relieved. He appeared to be absorbed in his task, his hands moving deftly over the wood. Broad, sure hands, with the lightest sprinkling of hairs on the backs of them, hands that would caress a woman with as much skill, as much sureness, as he used on the wood.

Paige's throat went dry at the thought and she forced her attention to the next sheet of plywood, the next scenery prop. Maybe it was the spring air that was making her a little crazy. Zach was a man who was dangerous to her sense of purpose.

He'd finished three more props in the time it had taken Paige to do one. Okay, so maybe men were faster at carpentry—but that didn't mean they were any more adept. Fortunately he didn't comment on the disproportionate rate of production.

She should be grateful for small favors.

He finished up the next prop and stood it beside the growing number lining one wall of the garage. He flexed his shoulders to get out the kinks, his muscles bunching and relaxing beneath the fabric of his shirt.

Paige swallowed hard and dragged her gaze away from the sight. "Want to take a break?" she asked. "I have some lemonade made, if you'd like a glass."

"You offer refreshments to your slave labor?" His grin was all male. "Yes, I'd like some. Need any help?" he added as she started toward the narrow breezeway that led to the kitchen.

"No, no help." What she needed was a moment alone, a moment to remind herself life could get complicated with this man.

And she didn't need complications.

When she returned a few moments later with two frosty glasses, Zach was standing beside her toolbox, studying her working outline of the scenery props—the prop description, along with its corresponding dance number penciled in beside it.

"This recital is a big undertaking," he said, leaning forward over the worksheet and scanning her notes. He shook his head as if he couldn't believe the amount of involvement she'd taken on. And this was only a small part of it.

"I prefer to think of it as a labor of love," she returned. He glanced up at that, and she held out a lemonade to him. "Icy cold," she promised.

His gaze stroked her face for the briefest of seconds, then he accepted the glass she offered him. Their hands brushed and Paige squeezed back a reaction to it. To him. Working side by side with the man had stirred up her awareness of everything about him.

"Then you're really dedicated to this dancing thing?"

She smiled softly. "I'm surprised you have to ask. I'd have thought it was obvious."

Zach leaned back against her workbench while Paige perched on an old step stool. He didn't answer for a moment, instead taking in this small sprite of a woman who surprised him day by day. She was five feet, plus an inch or two, of sheer determination and strength. And that he had to admire. "Perhaps not as obvious as it should have been," he said regretfully.

Her eyes were bright, her cheeks brushed with the heat of the afternoon. He'd vowed to keep his distance, but he wasn't sure that was possible, not when she was Jessie's dance teacher—something he himself had arranged. Not when she drew him to her as unerringly as a bee to sweet nectar.

"Well, I am. And determined to put on a recital this year, even though DanceWorks is still in its infancy.

The students have worked hard. They deserve to have their moment in the spotlight.''

"And so does the teacher." He saluted her with his glass of lemonade, then took a cooling swallow. It was tart, yet sweet. And refreshing on a warm afternoon.

He set down his half-empty glass and picked up her work plan. "You're going to need lots of help with this," he said, tapping a finger against the paper.

She looked up at him through a fringe of soft lashes. "I'm well aware of that."

Zach was sure he'd never seen eyes so mesmerizing. And so deep a man could wade into their depths and never want to surface. He recognized the danger in that, but he was fool enough to ignore it. "Well, then you'll need my help. I'll get these props organized for you, borrow a van from a friend of mine to transport them to the— Where is the recital supposed to be, anyway?"

Paige was certain she didn't want him to know. If it were possible, he'd *never* find out. She recognized his approach. She'd seen the same flash of fire in Stephen's eyes all too often—when he'd taken charge of something, something he was certain only he could do justice to. Paige would be forgotten to the planning as well as the execution.

"Don't you worry about it," she said, snapping the work list out of his hands, just before he could tuck it, folded, into the snug back pocket of his jeans.

"What are you doing?" he asked.

Her chin rose a determined three inches. "Saving myself."

His eyes narrowed. "Look, Paige. You need help to do this. I can be that help. Prop man and stage crew rolled into one. You'll need someone backstage to engineer everything."

"No one died and appointed you," she stormed, but he wasn't listening.

The fire in his eyes only heated a few more degrees. "Lights. What about lighting?"

"What about lighting? Zach, have you ever seen a stage revue, much less tried to put one together?"

"How hard can it be?"

"Damned hard, not to mention demanding and time-consuming. But the point is, this is *my* production. I'm in charge here, not you."

"Of course you're in charge."

The tone of that statement had the same effect as a chuck under the chin or a pat on the head. Zach meant well, she knew. But she also knew he'd take over her entire endeavor. It would no longer be hers, her dream, her vision. She wanted this success for herself. *Needed* it.

And that, she didn't think he could understand. He took charge of the lives of anyone he got close to. He barely gave little Jessie room to breathe; and she had no doubt he'd do the same with her if she gave him half an opportunity. She put the list she'd rescued from him on the workbench where it had been and smoothed a hand over it.

"In charge and perfectly capable of running the show," she said as if it were a mantra—or an incantation to ward off well-meaning, but dominating, men.

Zach wasn't sure what was behind Paige's feelings, but he recognized the intensity of them. He'd only wanted to help, but the lady obviously had other ideas.

"Fine," he said, "but I'm here if you need me." He'd have to be satisfied with that for now. He gave her a moment for his words to sink in, for the tenseness he'd noticed in her shoulders to ebb once again, for her pretty smile to surface.

And when it did, it wowed him. The woman was temptation in front of him, small and defiant. And so damned sexy that he wanted to kiss her.

But he wasn't sure she'd go for that, any more than she would let him help her with the recital. What had she said the other night, the night they'd shared a pizza, shared that kiss that had knocked them both for the proverbial loop?

That they shouldn't complicate things.

She was right—he knew it in his heart—still, it was damned hard to back away from the luscious temptation of her. "Come on," he said, his voice rough with regret. "We'd better finish getting these props built. That is, if you're going to let me at least do that."

The wariness returned to her beautiful eyes for a quick moment.

Why? he wondered. What did she fear?

Needing someone? Everyone needed someone, sometime.

Then his own thought brought him up short. He'd spent the past year convincing himself that was pure bunk, that except for Jessie, he needed no one.

But, in relation to Paige, his theory somehow seemed flawed.

He raised one eyebrow, waiting for her answer. She hesitated a moment more, as if fighting some disagreeable war inside her, then she picked up a hammer and handed it to him, and reached for the other one. "It'll go faster if we do it together."

Wasn't that what he'd told her in the first place?

Paige worked alongside the man, trying to ignore the heat of him so near her, the hunch of his wide shoulders as he bent over his work, the growing patches of dampness that decorated his shirt, making him look even more virile.

They brushed against each other more than once, and as always, it was electrifying to her. Did his body carry some sort of male charge? And why did she have to be so susceptible to it?

Paige felt as if she'd won the battle, but still had the war to fight.

Finally they had the last nail pounded into the last prop, and it was a good feeling. They both straightened and stretched their various aching joints.

"You're right. I needed your help or I'd have still been working on these at midnight," she said, conceding the point.

Zach smiled and brushed a loose wisp of Paige's hair away from her dewy-moist face, thinking how lovely it looked, how open, how fresh. "Oh, I wager you'd have gotten the job done, even without my help," he returned softly.

"Thanks for the vote of confidence. Considering how I sounded off awhile ago, it's nice of you."

"Oh, I'm nice all right. So nice I'll even buy you dinner tonight—after we clean up this mess."

"I should buy *you* dinner, but I'm afraid I can't tonight."

Disappointment shot through him. "Oh?"

Her shoulders slumped. "I'll be spending the evening on the phone trying to locate a seamstress to make costumes for the recital. I either have to come up with one fast—or start on them myself. And that, I'm afraid, ranks right up there with disaster. I don't have the talent to sew up a gunnysack."

"I see, then how about next week?" He wasn't to be easily dissuaded.

"If I find that seamstress, I'll think about it," she half promised.

"I guess I'll have to be satisfied with that."

He leaned down and gave her a soft brush across her pretty mouth, just a taste to satisfy his growing hunger. Just a sample, when he preferred a feast. But in that moment, she responded with a fire that was nearly his undoing.

Soft confusion reigned in her eyes when he drew away. But he didn't dare stay for more. Finding a push broom in the corner of the garage, he busied himself with cleaning up as he'd offered.

As he worked, an idea began to take shape in his head, a way to be certain Paige could keep that date with him for dinner. She might hate him for it, but it was a chance he had to take.

He wanted her all to himself for one night.

Paige hung up the phone and gave a deep sigh.

Another refusal.

What was she going to do? One by one she'd gone through the list of names Emily at Manley's Fabrics had given her. Four seamstresses, all highly touted by Emily, but all busy. Two were doing bridal gowns for large weddings. The other two were busy with prom dresses.

Spring was a busy season, something Paige hadn't bargained for when she'd set the recital date.

Some of the required costumes could be ordered from the various dance catalogs she got through the mail, if she ordered quickly, but most were her own creation. She picked up the sketches she'd made and thumbed through them.

A headache began to form behind her eyes and increased with each sketch she perused. Paige knew her talents did not extend to creating magic with her ancient Singer. Even if she coaxed and coddled and sweet-talked it, it had a way of jamming its gears somewhere along the route of every seam, something she suspected was more her doing than any fault of the machine's.

Maybe she could find a seamstress in Kansas City, she considered. There had to be at least one who wasn't doing weddings or proms. Or—heaven help her—other dance revues.

But could she find one quickly?

And—if she found one—how many fifty-mile trips into the city would it necessitate?

Then, too, there was the little matter of fittings. Could she get that someone to come to Libertydale to do them? Or would she have to transport her little troupe of pint-size dancers to *her?*

Paige dropped the sketches on the kitchen table, popped a mini pizza into the microwave for her dinner and set the timer. While she waited, she drummed her fingers on the cool blue tiles of the countertop. She had the sinking feeling that she'd be the one doing all the sewing.

That definitely eliminated dinner next week with Zach from her plans. Not that she'd decided to go. She hadn't. At least, not yet.

She was tempted.

More than tempted.

An evening with Zach—putting all thoughts of the recital out of her mind for a few hours—held a definite appeal.

Sitting across the table from him, listening to that low, rumbly laugh of his, seeing his smile soften those silvery-gray eyes held a *dangerous* appeal, a part of her clamored.

The quick brush of his lips across hers this afternoon had ignited her. Why? Because Zach was the first man she'd kissed since her marriage had ended? Or was it the powerful chemistry between them that refused to be denied?

Just then the microwave buzzer sounded, and Paige turned to take out her pizza. After she'd drowned herself in melted cheese and pepperoni, she would tackle painting the scenery props she and Zach had assembled. The problem of the costumes would have to wait another day.

Three days later, Paige was still minus one seamstress. She frowned down at the bolts of satin and tulle, thread and sequins stacked on her dining-room table. A cold chill shivered down her spine whenever she thought about picking up her scissors and cutting into the delicate fabric.

But time was running out. If she didn't come up with someone soon, her home would fast start resembling a garment factory.

Just then she heard the doorbell and knew that Jessie had arrived early for class again. She smiled. Jessie loved to come here, and Paige loved teaching her alone. Jessie's awkward little steps were growing surer. Her smile came quicker. And they were becoming friends.

There was only one problem. Jessie came with a daddy, a very sexy daddy, one who could make Paige's heart trip over itself.

She opened the door, expecting to find Jessie and Zach, but instead Ernestine was standing there, little Jessie clutching her hand.

"We're early," Ernestine announced.

Paige swallowed that small sliver of disappointment she wanted to deny, and invited the pair in. Of course Zach would still be at his office. Or finishing up in court. She'd scheduled Jessie's lesson for five, ahead of her other classes. Instead of being disappointed that the handsome hunk wasn't standing on her doorstep, she should feel relieved. The less she saw of Zach Delano, the better, she reminded herself sharply.

"Ernestine brought me," Jessie said, bounding through the doorway, carrying her dance bag in front of her like a proud banner. "But my daddy will be here later to pick me up."

"Ohhh?" Paige turned to Ernestine for confirmation of this.

The housekeeper nodded. "He said he'd do the honors. That way, I can get to work on those costumes you want made. You just give me the patterns and such and I'll—"

Paige stopped her. "Hold on a minute. What did you say?"

Ernestine repeated herself, but it hadn't been necessary. Paige had heard every word. Clearly. Zach had recruited his housekeeper to sew the costumes for her recital. But he hadn't seen fit to consult her about it beforehand.

The other day when they'd worked on the scenery props, he'd tried to take over. And now he'd done it again. Zach Take-Command Delano had come riding to her rescue when she hadn't asked for his help.

That take-charge attitude of his might be fine for the courtroom—commendable even—but not in Paige's life. And Paige intended to tell him just that—but later. Right now, she had a live-and-willing applicant for the job of costume maker. And she wasn't about to let this gift horse get away, not when she needed help so desperately.

"Ernestine, can you sew?" She wasn't sure why she was asking. Even if she couldn't sew a stitch, she had to be better than Paige.

"Of course I can sew, child," she said haughtily, indignant at having her talents questioned.

Paige didn't hesitate. "Then you've got the job."

She led the housekeeper into the dining room and introduced her to the miscellany spread out on her table, hoping the woman wouldn't bolt at the sight of the yards of fabric, not to mention thousands of tiny sequins in every color of the rainbow.

"Ernestine, are you sure you want to do this?"

Ernestine looked over the sketches of the costumes Paige had designed and the fabric swatches attached to each. She waved off the question. "Of course I want to do it, or I wouldn't have agreed."

Ernestine was a miracle. "Fine. Take the sketches home and go over them," she said. "Later we can find a time for you to come and measure the dancers for their costumes."

The woman nodded in agreement.

Once Ernestine had gone, trundling out the door loaded down with the designs, Paige turned to Jessie. She had a class to teach; later she'd decide how best to deal with Zach. She should be grateful to him for finding her a much-needed seamstress, and she would be—right after she'd given him what-for for his high-handed tactics.

She was determined to be her own woman, in charge of her own life, even if that meant making a few mistakes along the way. She didn't need a man to lean on, a man to come along and save her—no matter how irresistible the man might be.

And the sooner *this* man learned that about her, the better off her life would be.

"Are you ready to dance, Jessie?" Paige asked, tamping down her emotions. In no way did she want to take her feelings out on this little girl.

Jessie was fingering a pretty pink satin. "Can my costume be this one?" she asked Paige in a voice edged with a hint of awe.

The question caught Paige off guard. She hadn't decided yet whether Jessie would be in the recital. Paige wasn't at all sure the child would be ready to go onstage. But she didn't want to tell Jessie that. She couldn't crush her spirit.

She blamed Zach for this, as well—putting her in a vulnerable spot with his daughter.

"It's very pretty, isn't it?" Paige said as she ran a hand over the cool, smooth fabric. She understood what Jessie was feeling, and her heart squeezed out a beat. She would redouble her efforts with her, until Jessie could dance her number like a dream.

She held out her hand. "Come on, honey. If you're going to wear that costume, we've got to practice hard. That's what dancers do, you know."

Jessie gave the pink satin one last wistful glance, then smiled and took Paige's hand. "Yes, that's what dancers do," she repeated.

As Paige led Jessie downstairs to the studio, she felt as if an invisible net were tightening around her. She was being drawn into this family little by little.

She had decided to work even harder with Jessie to get her ready for the dance revue—which meant more time spent together with her. She'd just hired on Ernestine to make the costumes for her students. And Zach—Zach represented his own brand of danger. The most frightening kind. The kind that could make her lose her tenuous hold on the life she'd fought for and won, the independence she couldn't lose again.

Zach showed up just before the end of Jessie's lesson. He let himself in, motioned for them to go on with what they were doing and took a seat on the piano bench.

Jessie seemed more eager than ever to do her steps right, to show her daddy what she'd learned in Miss Paige's class, and Zach watched her avidly. Paige concentrated on Jessie in an effort to keep her fury at the man in check.

When the lesson was over and she'd dismissed her pupil, the child bounded over to Zach and gave him a giant hug around the neck. Paige had something else in mind for that part of his sexy anatomy.

But strangling the man would be too good for him.

After finding out how her lesson had gone, he released Jessie and glanced over at Paige, one eyebrow angled up inquiringly. "So, did you and Ernestine work everything out?"

Paige was ready to kill him. Only the fact that it would leave little Jessie fatherless kept her from doing it.

"Interesting you should ask, because that's just what I want to talk to you about," she said, each word clipped and barbed.

He got the message. "*Ouch*—did I step on the lady's toes?"

"With your usual combat boots."

A slow grin spread across his face.

Paige did not feel the same amusement.

"Why did I think you'd be greeting me with a hug and a great big thank you for finding you Ernestine?" he asked cheekily.

Why did most despots never see the people they ran over? Paige wondered silently. She did owe him a thank-you, a big one like he wanted. Ernestine had come along when she'd desperately needed a seamstress. But that was beside the point.

She opened her mouth to elucidate his transgression in full detail, then closed it again as Jessie bounded back into the room with her dance bag and her tennis shoes in her hand. She sat down at her father's feet to change out of her ballet slippers.

What Paige had to say to Zach Delano was not fit for the child's ears. "Maybe now is not the time to—" she cleared her throat "—explain my gratitude on the matter."

Zach smiled wryly. "Ah, well, maybe you can do that over dinner Saturday night."

"Dinner?"

"Yes. Don't you remember? You said if you found a seamstress, you'd have dinner with me."

Had she said that? She had. But she hadn't found a seamstress, Zach had found one *for* her. And that was the rub. Zach had taken over, interfered in her life—and she didn't accept that from anyone.

Not anymore.

If little Jessie hadn't found that soft spot in her heart, Paige would tell him just where he could go—and for how long. If she didn't need Ernestine and her services so desperately, he'd be out of her life in the bat of an eye.

Zach had effectively boxed her in—not only with dinner but also with his being firmly and unalterably rooted in her life.

"So, how about it? Saturday night?" When she didn't answer, he went on. "I have a special surprise, so wear something . . . fetching."

Chapter Six

Paige spent as much of her time trying to figure out what Zach's special surprise for the evening was as she did on her anger at him.

She'd tried to hang on to that anger, but the fact remained, Zach had done her a big favor in finding Ernestine—and she couldn't lose sight of that.

He'd been pushy, yes. He hadn't bothered to discuss it with her beforehand, definitely. But as she and Ernestine went over all the costume ideas this morning, Paige's fury was slowly replaced with relief. The woman was a godsend, despite Zach's deception.

By Saturday afternoon, her thoughts centered on what she'd wear for this special evening out with him. Once again he hadn't deemed fit to let her in on what he had planned. She'd tried to pry it out of Ernestine, but the woman had pleaded innocence. If she knew, she wasn't telling.

Paige rummaged through her closet, searching for something that seemed to fit into the category of special. Nothing did.

Except—

A small smile edged her lips as she reached to the back of the closet and pulled out the perfect dress. She'd never worn it and had almost forgotten she had it.

Would Zach consider it *fetching* enough for whatever he had in mind?

She held it up to herself, scrutinizing her reflection in the cheval mirror. What she saw worried her. The neck was a little bare. So was the back . . . completely. And the clingy, midnight-blue fabric showed off her feminine curves with dangerous definition.

Maybe Zach wouldn't notice, she thought hopefully.

And maybe pigs could fly.

With a low groan she tossed the thing across the bed and went off to take her shower.

An hour later, she was ready—almost.

She still had her nerves to get under some kind of shaky control. She hadn't dressed up and gone out for an evening since . . . *forever*, but she needed to somehow muster the aplomb to look as if this was an everynight occurrence. That this date with Zach was no big deal, when in reality, her heart was doing a syncopated tap number behind her ribs.

She should be keeping a goodly distance from Zach Delano. Instead, she was going out to dinner with him and—heaven only knew what else.

Zach tucked the ballet tickets into his breast pocket, hoping they would be enough to make Paige forget her anger at him—at least for tonight. The tickets had been hard to come by on such short notice, but he knew Paige would be thrilled at the chance to see the performance.

As for himself, a little exposure to the arts couldn't hurt. Maybe it would get him in the right frame of mind for this recital thing Paige and his young daughter were so excited about. But mostly he hoped it would appease Paige.

Maybe he'd overstepped his bounds in finding her a seamstress before clearing it with her first. And maybe he'd come on a little too strong in her garage, trying to tell her the best way to assemble those props. But was that any reason for her to refuse his well-intentioned help on the recital?

She needed him. Paige just didn't want to admit it. And he wondered why.

Straightening his red power tie, the one he wore when he had a challenging date in the courtroom, he climbed out of the Bronco and headed for Paige's front door. Tonight he felt the same way he did when he faced the steeliest judge on the bench with a touch-and-go case to win.

Nervous.

He was glad he'd remembered to bring flowers. Women liked flowers...and Ernestine would never miss the few he'd filched from her prize garden. After all, it was for a good cause—*his* cause. Drawing a deep, steadying breath, he rang the bell.

A moment later Paige opened the door, and Zach held out the bouquet to her, certain he couldn't get his voice past the large lump in his throat. Paige looked so damned sexy in that blue dress, she took his breath away. And very nearly his sanity. It hugged and cupped and bared the most enticing parts of her.

"Flowers! Thank you," she said, giving them a sniff. "I'll just put them in water. Come in," she invited.

He didn't want her to leave the room, he didn't want her out of his sight. "I'll help."

She frowned. "Zach...I'm perfectly capable of—" She stopped midsentence, realizing he was looking at her with an appreciative male gleam in his eyes. It was the dress. She never should have worn the dress.

She tugged upward on the low-dipped bodice.

"Don't...touch a thing," he said. "You look *terrific*."

The way he eyed her up and down sent a tingle through her...and made her feel every inch a woman. It had been a long time since a man had made her feel so feminine. But never, she was certain, with quite the tingle Zach was capable of producing in her.

She resisted the urge to hide behind the bouquet of spring daisies he'd brought her and wished there were another dress in her closet she could hastily change into. But she knew there wasn't.

Not one that would do justice to a man decked out in a dark silk suit and a snowy-white shirt that fitted him to a "T" and made him achingly handsome.

She let out a slow, ragged breath.

She'd have a fine time explaining to him how she felt about his interference in her life when just the sight of him had her head spinning and her senses reeling.

Perhaps later...when she was more in command of herself. Later...when Zach didn't affect her with the impact of a head-on collision in a bumper car, she could tell him what she had to say.

"I have a vase somewhere," she said as she headed toward the kitchen.

Zach followed her graceful exit with his gaze.

And a groan.

The back of the dress was as bare as the front.

Either coming or going she had him in a world of trouble tonight. He could see her peering into a cabinet, searching for a vase. His gut tightened and his pulse pounded.

Forcing his attention away, he jammed his hands into his pockets and glanced round her small living room for something to occupy his sight, if not his thoughts. He'd always considered himself a man of strong will, but tonight he'd have to call on all his powers of restraint.

When he turned around again, Paige was placing the vase of flowers in a small, niched opening between the kitchen and dining room, then she turned and started toward him, her walk so slow, so decidedly sexy, he felt as if he were fragmenting inside.

He'd thought he could handle a simple date with her, keep it casual, the way he preferred to keep things these days, but he wasn't sure that was possible where Paige was concerned. And that frightened the hell out of him.

"Where is this restaurant?" she asked once they were finally on their way.

"A little café in Kansas City I thought you might enjoy." A far too intimate little café, now that he thought about it.

"Is that the surprise? Dinner? The café?"

"No. The surprise comes after."

"After?" There was a rising note of curiosity in her voice, which he didn't intend to accommodate. At least not yet.

Later, he would tell her—when he could devote all his attention to watching her green eyes light up, her pretty mouth curve into a wide smile of delight.

Besides, *later* he might need those tickets as an enticement to get her to talk to him—after she was through drilling him about Ernestine.

He glanced over at her. That seductive mouth of hers was pursed into a pout so provocative it could tie a man's libido into a major knot. "Zach Delano, you're going to keep me in suspense all through dinner?''

She was clearly not pleased at the prospect.

Paige liked having her way, it seemed. And he supposed it would be a small price to pay to give it to her. But it made him wonder why it was so important to her.

Had she once been denied her own mind?

With all the strength and determination that bristled inside her, it was hard to believe that anyone with a viable IQ would have risked the wrath of this woman.

He pulled out onto the interstate, set the cruise control and eased back in his seat. ''Okay, how about I tell you *at* dinner? Good enough?'' That was as far as he'd go. Bottom line.

''Deal,'' she answered, then laughed, and Zach loved the sound, the way it whispered up from her throat and wrapped around his senses.

The conversation on the ride into the city was more relaxed once she'd secured the upper hand—or at least what she perceived as the upper hand. She talked about Jessie and how well she was doing in her one-on-one lessons with Paige. She asked Zach about his cases—and he realized it had been a long time since a woman had asked him about his work, his day. Janet always had—but Janet was gone.

It was a touch of intimacy he hadn't fully known was missing from his life.

Until Paige reminded him.

He found himself telling her anecdotes about his work—just to enjoy the provocative tilt of her head when she listened, the way her voice rose at the end of a question she asked, her smile that sprang so easily to her lips.

Smiling was something else that had been missing from his life, Jessie being the only one who could elicit one from him. Until Paige made him smile.

It seemed no time at all before the lights of the city came into view, glittering like a jeweled sea ahead of them.

The restaurant was tucked away in a quiet corner of the city's historic garment district, with big green awnings and brass lanterns lighting the entrance. Paige declared it quaint and wondered how he'd found it.

"I came here once with friends. It's a well-kept secret in Kansas City, one the natives don't like to share. They want to keep the ambience and delicious food all for themselves," he explained, leading her inside.

They found a table easily in an intimate little corner. But at the moment, Zach would have preferred a well-lighted bus stop. Paige had every one of his senses fired up to a kindling temperature, and he doubted there would be any relief for the night.

He concentrated on the menu and choosing a wine, settling finally on something light and delicate. They ordered dinner, as well, both of them deciding on the house favorite, a specially prepared smoked salmon steak.

"To the first of many famous Paige Hanford recitals," Zach said, proposing a toast when the wine had arrived. "May it go off without a hitch."

Or one of her little cherubs throwing up in the wings, Paige thought to herself. She met his gaze with her own. "That's sweet, Zach. I feel like the recital's officially an event now." She took a slow sip of wine, but her gaze remained locked with his.

The candlelight had turned his eyes silvery—and incredibly seductive. So was the restaurant, the whole evening. And she was falling under some kind of spell. She wanted to shake herself to dispel it.

Their food arrived, and Zach ate hungrily. Paige relaxed somewhat and enjoyed the delicious dinner and easy conversation. Zach ordered dessert, a sinfully rich chocolate confection Paige preferred to watch him eat, enjoying it vicariously. She hadn't kept her lithe dancer shape by indulging often.

"Mmm. Just a bite—you've got to try just a bite." Zach balanced a gooey portion on the end of his fork and held it temptingly out to her.

She laughed. "Okay, but just one."

She grasped his wrist to guide the fork to her mouth. Paige hadn't realized how sensual it could be to have a man feed her warm, decadent chocolate. Or how intimate the gesture.

His wrist beneath her fingertips was sinewy strength and heat. A pulse beat there, strong and sure, reminding her Zach was a very real, flesh-and-blood man and she was likely playing with fire.

She released her hold on him and tasted the bite. It was as sinful as the man seated across from her, every bit a temptation.

"Good?" he inquired.

"Yes." Her voice was a hoarse whisper. "Wonderful." She stole her gaze away from his, fearing he'd see the reflection of his effect on her there in her eyes.

Zach could be a threat to her newfound freedom if she gave him the power. If she lost her heart to him. And that she didn't dare do.

"I should get a few dozen take-out orders," he said, once he'd polished off his dessert. "I have the feeling I'm going to be a starving man soon, with all the work you gave Ernestine. I won't get a cake or pie for the duration."

Paige hoped that was true—as punishment for what he'd done. She should have a word with Ernestine. Fatten up little Jessie, but let the big man beg. "You only have yourself to blame for that, Zach Delano," she said with a definite arch of one eyebrow.

He gave her his best beguiling smile. "Now, Paige, I thought you'd be happy with Ernestine."

She sighed and narrowed her eyes at him. "I am. The woman is a lifesaver, but that's not the point, Zach."

"And what exactly is the point?" He'd leaned forward across the table, his attention focused firmly on her.

Paige didn't know if she could make him understand, but she had to try. It was the perfect time. They were alone, without little Jessie in attendance. "The point is, I'm a big girl and I can handle my life myself."

"I see."

No, Paige doubted he did. No one but she could know the insidiousness of Stephen's attempts to control her, own her. No one could know how much it had cost her in self-esteem and confidence, through her four-year marriage to him. How her dreams had died slowly day by day, year by year.

He'd made her doubt herself, every quality she owned. He'd done it because he was afraid he'd lose her. But that was not an excusable reason to smother someone, take away their own inner support system. What Stephen had done was wrong.

Zach saw the faint tremor in Paige's lower lip and he wanted to kiss it away, he wanted to take her into his arms and keep her safe. Someone had hurt her, hurt her badly. He wanted to know who, why.

He wanted to make it right—if he could.

"Paige, tell me what's wrong. I realize I shouldn't have talked to Ernie about the costumes before discussing it with you first. I know that now, but that's not all of it, is it?"

That didn't explain why she wouldn't accept his help.

"No, you shouldn't have gone behind my back, as if I'm not capable, as if—" She broke off when she felt tears sting her eyes.

She was blowing what he'd done out of all proportion. Because of Stephen. Because of what he'd done to her in the past. But she couldn't seem to stop her fury. Half of it was at Zach, but half was out of fear that history could repeat itself—with Zach.

He was strong, forceful, used to having his way in the courtroom. And she'd seen firsthand how protective he could be of Jessie.

"Paige, I wasn't indicating you weren't capable..." That was it, he was sure. Someone had doubted her abilities, made her doubt herself.

"Maybe...maybe you weren't," she said, her voice tremulous. She looked up at him. Her wide green eyes were smoky with pain. "Zach, all my life I had someone looking after me. I never got the chance to stand on my own two feet, tell the world what I, Paige Hanford, could do. Or show them. My father treated me like his little princess when I was growing up. I wanted to do something with my dancing career. I...wanted to go to New York for some special tryouts, but...but my father didn't want me to leave home for the big city. Anything could happen to me, he'd said."

She paused and took a deep breath. The pain was still there, shimmering softly in her eyes, and Zach hated to see it.

"After that disappointment, I...I married Stephen. Too late I realized he was a man very much like my father, except...except that Stephen could be cruel. What my father had done, he'd done out of love. Stephen did it out of the belief that I was his. Like property—his house, his car, his wife."

Zach's fist clenched and unclenched on the table. He could understand her father's fears. He had them for Jessie. But Stephen... He didn't know the man, but he hated him.

"Zach, for the first time in my life I'm standing alone, making my own decisions, learning to trust in my own judgment. My school and this dance recital are a test of what I can do. Me, myself, alone..."

His fingers reached for hers across the table, not in any possessive way, just touching, so she'd know they were there to cling to if that's what she needed. But Paige, he was certain, wouldn't take them. She needed to stand on her own.

"Then some big jerk came along and tried to tell you how to build a few props, hired you a seamstress without consulting you first. I'm surprised you're even speaking to me," he said.

His heart turned over when he saw the beginnings of a smile brush her soft mouth. It was a hesitant smile, but it was a smile.

And Zach hoped he was home free.

"I'm glad you told me," he said. He could see now why she guarded her independence so fiercely. She was testing life on her own for the very first time, then he'd come along and tried to take over in his usual take-the-bull-by-the-horns manner. "I'll do my best to stay out of your way," he promised. "But, Paige, I want you to know I'm there if you need help."

He saw her shoulders stiffen a little at that. Needing help, his or anyone's, wasn't something she'd admit to readily—if ever, he thought.

And that bothered him.

He'd meant what he'd promised, he'd stay out of her way, let her run her own show—but he wasn't sure he could stay out of her life.

If the other bothered him, this scared the bejesus out of him. He was afraid that in one unguarded moment he might tumble headlong into love with Paige Hanford.

"Tickets to *Swan Lake*!"

Zach's perfidy was forgotten, and Paige hated the fact that she could be bought so easily. But the ballet in Kansas City's old, restored Folly Theater was too much for her to ignore.

Considering the unladylike screech she'd emitted, she was glad Zach had waited until they were safely out of the restaurant to show them to her. She snatched the tickets out of his hands, wanting to hold them in her own, revel in the luxury of them.

Zach was laughing at her indulgently, the way an adult would laugh at a child whose every wish had been fulfilled on Christmas morning.

"Oh, Zach, you couldn't have given me a nicer surprise," she confessed.

"Well, if we're going to see this performance, we'd better be on our way. The theater's not far from the restaurant. Do you want to walk or take the car?"

"Let's walk," she answered without a hesitation. "It's a beautiful night." And she wanted to savor every moment of it, enjoy it, treasure it.

He found the small of her back as he guided her along the sidewalk. It was a casual touch, yet intimate in the softness of the night. The glow of street lamps lit their way. The mellow strains of Kansas City jazz drifted out from a dimly lit club they passed and mingled with the sounds of the light street traffic.

Paige soaked up the ambience of the night and the heat of the man beside her. For a while they didn't speak, just enjoyed. And anticipated what was to come.

Ahead she could see the lights of the theater. Patrons in their evening finery hurried toward the entrance. "Oh, Zach, I'm so excited. Can't you just feel the thrill of it?"

Zach smiled. "You really love this dance stuff." His gaze slid over her. "Maybe you can show me the excitement." He'd like to share it with her, understand what it was that made her so passionate about it.

"I've never thought of anything but dance since I was Jessie's age," she said, her voice soft, a little breathless. "And yes, I'd like to show you the excitement."

He caught her hand and entwined his fingers through hers. They were trembling. And she was glowing. He tugged her gently to a stop. She gazed up at him, soft confusion reigning in her eyes.

"I just have to kiss you," he said.

Those eyes widened. Her lips parted and he brushed his mouth across them, capturing all their heat and fire. Their passion.

"Just a taste to get me through to intermission," he murmured. "They do have intermission at these things, don't they?"

"They do."

He kissed her once more, a savoring kiss. Slow and sensual. It warmed his blood, heated his senses. And he felt her respond.

Because of Paige, because he knew she wouldn't want to miss a moment of the performance, he drew away, ending the kiss. "We're going to be late," he reminded her. He touched a finger to her bottom lip, his nobility killing him.

Paige returned to the here and now. Zach's kiss had the power to make her forget the dance she loved, make her forget that she wanted to see this performance more than she wanted to breathe. "Yes," she said. "We'd better go."

There was an excitement in the theater that was palpable, as if it had a life of its own. Paige fairly dragged Zach down the aisle to their seats. The moment they reached their row, she knew the seats were good ones. They had a great view of the stage, close enough to see the beautiful movement of the dancers, yet far enough back for reality to recede, for it to seem like a dream that she was caught up in, not a performance.

Perhaps that was the way it was with her and Zach. He was a dream she was caught up in. She'd forgotten they were real people, with lives of their own that needed to be played out. Separately. Not together.

She shoved the thought aside as the music began and the house lights dimmed. She didn't want to think about reality. Tonight wasn't a time for it. Tonight was a time for dreams.

She'd promised to make Zach feel the excitement. She leaned close to him, their shoulders touching. The curtain rose and Paige's throat caught. The dancers swept on stage.

In a hushed whisper she explained the ballet. Zach listened, entranced, not by her story of the beautiful ballet, but by the sweetness of Paige's voice, soft as fine velvet against his ear. Her breath was warm, feathering against his senses until he was close to distraction. He could imagine her whispering other words to him in the dark of the night, seductive words, sweet and low and desperate with need.

Need for him.

The theater felt warm—he felt even warmer. He yanked on his noose of a tie to loosen it and struggled to keep his attention on what Paige was saying about Prince Siegfried vowing to kill some guy named Rothbart, but it was hard.

All he could think about was Paige.

Her body was as delicate as any of the dancers on stage. Poetry, he'd thought the first time he'd seen her. And he thought so still. She was softness and beauty, sensual heat and wild fascination.

And he wanted to make love to her.

The houselights came up for intermission. People rose from their seats, moving toward the plush lobby to see and be seen. Zach was more in favor of skipping the second half and stealing away to some private place with Paige.

But he knew he couldn't. Taking her away from the ballet she was so enamored with would be unfair to her. He suggested they try the lobby for a glass of wine.

"So, what do you think?" Paige asked when he handed a goblet of wine to her.

"I think you would make as beautiful a dancer as any in the production."

She blushed. "I meant, what do you think about the ballet?"

Paige suspected Zach was bored. She'd seen him loosen his tie and squirm in his seat. Not all men were intrigued by the arts, and she appreciated Zach's gesture in coming here tonight. He'd wanted to please her—and that made her feel very special indeed.

"I think I'd like to see that Rothbart guy get his," he said with his sexy grin that could curl her toes.

"Ah, so you *were* paying attention."

"Of course," he lied. Zach had been paying attention only to Paige, but he didn't tell her that.

Just then, the houselights dipped twice, the signal for them to return to their seats. Zach touched a hand to her waist and led her back inside, wondering how he would ever make it through to the end with the most desirable woman in the theater beside him.

Chapter Seven

Paige was in a daze on the drive back to Liberty-dale, not from the wine but from the ballet. Her head was full of ideas for costumes, dance routines. She'd even stolen her gaze away from the dancing to take note of musical scores and lighting. Her little recital could never compare with the beauty of *Swan Lake,* of course, but she had picked up a pointer or two she intended to employ.

Zach had made the evening special.

For her.

Even now he was giving her time to flutter down to earth slowly. He hadn't spoken a word on their walk back to the Bronco, just held her hand and let her dream of swans and golden crowns and handsome princes.

He was quiet now, glancing over at her occasionally with a look or a smile as he drove. With a soft sigh she settled back in her seat, imagining Zach as the gallant Siegfried and herself the beautiful swan queen. With one major difference—Zach was her prince only for the remainder of the evening.

Princes didn't translate into reality. Life wasn't a fairy tale in which people lived happily ever after.

"Penny for your thoughts," he said finally.

She smiled. "Only a penny?"

"The horrors of inflation. Okay, what will a buck seventy-five buy these days?"

She laughed, then glanced away. "I was thinking that this was a very nice evening, that the ballet was special and..."

"And?"

Paige didn't want to tell him that she might be falling in love with him. Or how much that possibility frightened her. Tomorrow would be time enough to deal with the reality of it, time enough to convince herself it wasn't really happening, that she'd only been caught up in tonight, the ballet...and fairy tales. "And that you were very sweet to think of it," she finished instead.

"Sweet?" He looked affronted.

"You have a problem with sweet?"

What Zach had felt about Paige all evening could hardly be deemed sweet, not by any stretch of the imagination. The woman tested his powers of male endurance to the limit. He gave her a slow grin. "Let's just say it's not a term often used in reference to me."

"Oh."

He returned his eyes to the road, preferring the sight of concrete to the tempting view of Paige, soft and feminine in the shadowy light of the car's interior. He was far too aware of her, seated mere inches away. Her provocative scent...her radiating body heat...her very presence.

The highway home had never seemed so long.

"Care to put on some music?" he asked as he indicated a supply of tapes he often listened to when he drove.

"Yes, that would be nice." She spent several moments searching through his collection, then popped one into the stereo system.

Immediately the car was flooded with sound, something slow and sultry, a tape he didn't remember he had. But unerringly Paige had found it. He wanted to groan at the hot, desperate wailing of a trombone, feeling a strange affinity to the instrument. As tortured as the sounds that came from its deepest core.

That's what Paige was doing to him, had done from the first time he'd laid eyes on her. She turned him inside out—without even trying.

The tape played and Paige hummed along with it, her voice as low and sultry as the music, her head thrown back against the headrest, the creamy curve of her neck exposed and vulnerable. He ached to touch his lips to its silky paleness, absorb the beauty of the sound that tore from it, plaguing his libido. She was lost to the music, and he was lost to her.

He barely remembered the miles he ate up. He only knew he was on fire by the time he reached Paige's driveway. When he killed the engine, she turned to glance at him, her green eyes vibrant and glittery in the moonlight.

"Oh, Zach, this has been a perfect evening." Her voice that had haunted him all the way home was feathery and soft.

"Yes," he replied. Only his need for Paige had made it torture.

He didn't dare take her inside—he'd make love to her without the slightest apology to his conscience. He'd never wanted a woman as much as he wanted Paige. He drew her to him and she came, all too willingly. He wished she'd resist—because he couldn't.

Her mouth was warm and supple when he took it. He kissed it brandingly, possessively, selfishly. She melted beneath him, her body curved to his, fitting to him as easily as she had in his fevered imaginings.

Paige was what he'd been restless for—but hadn't fully realized until tonight. And that was why she was so dangerous. She wasn't a woman he could satisfy himself with and then walk away. Paige was more than lust in the night, she was temptation in the day—and all his days to come if he gave in to that temptation.

Paige could barely breathe from the heat of Zach. He swamped her senses, his body hard against hers, his hands holding, caressing, urgent in their need. She understood that need; she felt its ravages, too. Her lips parted, and his tongue found entrance into her mouth, searching, tasting. She could only cling to him, wanting more of him.

The silk fabric of her dress was little barrier for his fingertips as he brushed them over the fullness of her breasts. Her nipples hardened in response at the erotic rub of silk against skin, Zach's touch against her fevered body. She let out a small sound of pleasure, knowing this had to end, yet wanting it to continue. She was falling in love with Zach and she couldn't allow herself to.

Not until she was strong, until she was secure in who she was and what she could accomplish. And tonight, against the power of Zach, the way he could make her respond so easily, as if she didn't have a will of her own, she knew she hadn't reached that place of certainty yet.

Feeling as if her heart were ripping, she drew back from the circle of his arms, away from the magnet of his body. A shudder shivered up from her throat and she found her voice. "No, Zach . . ."

Zach stopped her words with a soft kiss to her quivery bottom lip. "I know," he murmured. "I'm not sure if what we do to each other is good, but it's certainly overwhelming. Come on," he said, "I'll walk you to your door."

This time Paige allowed him to because she didn't trust her legs to hold her up.

* * *

Zach let a smile creep to his lips as Jessie pirouetted around the room, performing *jetés* and *arabesques,* trying to catch a glimpse of herself in the mirror he'd just put up in her playroom. All he had left to do was install the *barre* and she could practice to her heart's content.

There was only one problem—deciding on the proper height of the thing so as not to stress Jessie's young limbs.

He could do with a word of advice from Paige, but Paige was a temptation he couldn't afford. After their evening together the other night, he knew that.

Besides, how hard could this be?

He yanked out a yard of metal tape measure and pressed it to the wall at the side of the mirror, made a mark with his pencil, then let the tape snap back in its holder. Raising the *barre* level with the mark, he eye-balled it for height.

Perfect!

"That doesn't look right, Daddy."

Jessie had stopped dancing and stood watching him, her glasses slipped down on her nose, her tiny lips pursed.

"It doesn't, huh?" Zach gave the thing a critical glance.

"Nope."

"Are you sure?"

She planted her hands on her slim hips. "I think we should ask Miss Paige."

"Naw, punkin', we can do this ourselves. I'll get it right." He moved the *barre* an inch or two. "There. Better?"

Jessie wasn't to be swayed. She shook her head, her ponytail dancing in stubborn insistence, and let out a sigh that bespoke exasperation.

Zach felt like a man trapped. By a four-year-old and a woman who'd turned their life upside down in a few short weeks. He cast a frown at the *barre*, then lowered it to the floor and let out his own sigh of exasperation.

"She'll come and help, Daddy. I know she will. Miss Paige will show you where it should be."

Paige seemed to be his daughter's answer to everything these days, all she ever talked about. Jessie adored Paige, imitated her walk, her hairstyle. Even her stance now, hands on hips, chin raised in defiance, was Paige replicated.

She'd lent herself as role model to a little girl in desperate need of one. Jessie had been lost, and Paige had become her friend.

"Can we call her, Daddy? Can we? Can we?"

This was his doing. He'd put Paige in their life. In Jessie's and in his. And now he didn't know what to do about it.

He tipped Jessie's glasses back up on her pert nose.

She looked so much like Janet, with her dark curls and big, blue eyes, he thought, and that brought a downpour of guilt on his broad shoulders, guilt that he'd failed Jessie by failing Janet, failed to keep her safe from harm.

He might have lost Jessie, too, that night, a fear that gripped him whenever he saw his daughter looking soft and vulnerable. It was a risk you took when you loved someone too much, a risk he couldn't take again—not with Paige, not with any woman.

The attraction was there between them, hot and vital and overwhelming, something Paige was fighting against as much as he. She wasn't any more ready for this love thing than Zach. She was trying to find herself again after a destructive marriage, trying to find her own place in the world. He should let her do that, and perhaps in doing so, would save himself.

He tugged Jessie to him. She'd reached out to Paige, and for that, he was glad. Jessie had come a long way since Janet's death. Farther than himself. She was learning to trust again, to love again, where he didn't dare.

Jessie's friendship with Paige was important, and he couldn't take that from her. He glanced down at his daughter. "Maybe Miss Paige wouldn't mind giving us a pointer or two," he said.

Jessie exclaimed with glee.

"Zach, you spoil that child."

Paige glanced around Jessie's playroom filled with every conceivable toy, a collection of dolls and stuffed animals to rival that of a major toy store, and more in the frilly little-girl bedroom she glimpsed just beyond.

Then there was the mirror Zach had installed that ran nearly wall-to-wall and up to within a few inches of the ceiling. It stopped just short of the hand-painted border of dancing ballerinas that encircled the room. More ballerinas graced one wall in a wide mural, all of it having taken someone hours to paint.

"Your handiwork?" she asked Zach.

He shook his head. "Hardly. I hired a painter from the Art Institute in Kansas City. There's a similar one in Jessie's bedroom—storybook characters that are all her favorites."

Paige circled the room with her gaze. "And in spite of all this spoiling, Jessie has managed to remain a sweet child. It's unbelievable. You're unbelievable."

"I want my daughter to be happy. Happy and safe and loved. Is that a crime?"

"No, Zach. But smothering her is."

He stood in front of her, arms crossed over his broad chest, his head cocked toward her. "Do you think that's what I'm doing?"

Paige thought he was more than capable of it, suspected he was trying to make it up to Jessie—in every way that he could—for her not having a mother. His motives might be good, but the result could be most damaging. She knew what it was like to be smothered for all the right reasons, as well as the wrong. And Zach, she suspected, could get lost in his own best intentions.

"You try so hard to protect her—from everything," she said. "Let Jessie be a little girl, let her be free."

"I can't do that, Paige."

His silver-gray eyes shuttered closed, but before they did she'd glimpsed the pain in them. She'd shared her past with him, the painful parts as well as some of the happier times, but Zach hadn't done the same. "Why, Zach? What is it you're so afraid of?" Her voice was soft, questioning, insistent.

He rubbed a hand over the back of his neck. When he spoke, his voice was low, husky with emotion. "I don't want to lose Jessie the way I lost..."

"Jessie's mother?"

"Yes. Janet was killed in a car accident. Jessie was with her that night, but she was okay, unhurt. I should have been able to protect them. I should have been able to..."

"Keep an accident from happening? Zach, no one can do that. You can't wrap a protective shell around someone you love to keep them safe."

His hand massaged his neck again. "I don't agree. If I'd been more attentive, on guard..."

Zach might have said more but just then Jessie bounded into the room, effectively cutting off further conversation. She and Ernestine had been to the farmer's market to buy strawberries, and Jessie was ecstatic to find Paige there.

"The little mite was in a big hurry to get back here to see Miss Paige," Ernestine announced. "She couldn't wait for me to pick out the fattest ones, so what I got will have to do for tonight's shortcake.''

A smile touched Zach's lips as he gazed at Jessie, then glanced over at his housekeeper. ''I'm sure they'll be fine, Ernie.''

Ernestine gave a doubtful frown, then turned and trundled back down the stairs to stem her berries.

Jessie clasped Paige's hand and showed her Zach's attempt at installing the *barre*. ''I told my daddy you'd come and help. I told him you'd show him how to put it up for us. He wasn't doing it right,'' she divulged in a knowing, sometimes-daddies-aren't-too-smart tone.

Paige gave a half smile. ''Well then, I guess I'll just have to show him how to do it right, won't I?''

Jessie giggled, and Paige exchanged a glance with Zach, who handed her a tape measure and nodded his approval for her to have a go at it.

Jessie didn't want to leave Paige's side, Zach noted as he observed their two heads bent together as if deep in consultation. He didn't intrude, but watched them work from his vantage point across the room, prepared with his electric screwdriver for when the two were through with their own fact-gathering measurements.

They were quite the pair, Paige with her tawny hair that begged to be touched and Jessie's dark locks that Ernestine had tucked into a ponytail this morning.

Paige's frame was slender and lithe as she bent to measure, then turned to smile or laugh with her young sidekick. It was plain to see that Jessie worshiped the woman, needed her—he only wished he wasn't beginning to believe he needed her, as well. To make him smile the way he used to... to share things with, like dreams, fears... to warm his bed at night....

Just then, Paige turned around to beckon him and his trusty screwdriver closer. Quickly he schooled his expression so she couldn't read what had been on his mind. If she'd noticed, she'd given no indication, and he was glad.

"I need one bracket here," she said. "This high for now. Then as Jessie grows, you can adjust it higher."

If Jessie's passion for dance continued, he thought. For now, it showed no signs of abatement. Neither did his attraction to Paige.

She stood next to him while he fit the bracket to the wall, her soft fragrance playing havoc with his powers of concentration. She smelled like spring flowers—lilacs, he thought. She reached out a hand to steady the bracket for him and their shoulders touched, their arms entwined. He felt the press of her hip against his, soft against hard. It was all he could do to breathe, to hold his hands steady.

"There," he said when he had the bracket secured, the word coming out like a gasp for air.

Her face was so close he could lean over and kiss the satin of her lips. He wished he understood their lure—so that he could better guard against it. Her mouth parted slightly as if anticipating the taste of him. Her breath was so warm, her body so tempting... But

Jessie was in the room. With a sigh he drew back. "I'd better do the other bracket," he said on a groan.

She sighed. "Of course."

Paige stood back, allowing Zach to do the other side by himself. She was shaking too much to help him. Zach affected her with the same impact as a hurtling meteorite. She'd wanted him to kiss her, could almost feel the press of his mouth to hers. Drawing a deep breath, she tried to get hold of her senses.

She smiled over at Jessie, turning her attention to the child and off her disturbing daddy. Jessie had barely left Paige's side since she'd returned with Ernestine. Had the little girl noticed the fireworks that sparked between her and Zach?

"Finished," he said when he'd finally set the *barre* in place. "Look okay?"

Paige gave it an admiring glance. "I pronounce it perfect."

Jessie let out a cheer and raced over to try it out.

"She's a very lucky little girl," Paige whispered with a soft smile when Zach came to stand beside her. "I'd have loved to have had my very own room to practice in when I was Jessie's age."

"So I spoil her a little. I don't see why that's so wrong."

Paige heard the controlling tone in his voice and backed off from saying more. She doubted she could change his mind, or his steely determination that since Jessie was *his* daughter, *he'd* decide what was best for her.

They watched Jessie for a while longer, then Ernestine called the child downstairs to sample the cookies she'd just taken out of the oven.

"Strawberry shortcake *and* cookies? Zach, Ernie is so busy doing things for you and Jessie. I don't see how she's going to have time to sew costumes, too," Paige said. "Maybe I should scout around for someone to help her with them. You know, an assistant."

"Only if you have a death wish. Ernie would not take kindly to an assistant. She'd be insulted at the idea."

Paige frowned. "The last thing I want to do is make her angry. I need her—desperately."

"Then don't suggest an assistant." He paused. "Speaking of costumes—Ernie's been anxious to get started on Jessie's."

Paige studied her hands for a moment, giving her fingertips undue interest.

"Paige . . ."

She avoided looking up, knowing she would read the question on his face, and she wasn't sure of an answer. She'd spent a lot of time lately trying to decide just where to place Jessie in the recital, what number, either tap or ballet, that she might have down pat enough by that night. So far the verdict was neither.

"Paige, she *is* going to be in the recital, isn't she?"

Paige would decide on a number for Jessie. She couldn't leave her out of the revue, not when the child's little heart was set on it. "Jessie? Yes. Yes, of course, she'll be in the recital."

Zach studied Paige's face. She'd hesitated ever so slightly, but he hadn't missed it. Or the unwarranted scrutiny she'd given to her hands before that. He wanted to know why—and he was sure as hell going to find out.

His spine stiffened. "You don't think she's accomplished enough, do you?" he said with all the defiance of a mother bear defending her offspring. He wouldn't allow Paige, *anyone*, to hurt his daughter.

Paige spread her hands. "Look, Zach, I said Jessie would have a number in the recital, and she will."

"Tap or ballet?"

"I— Don't pin me down. I haven't decided for sure yet."

He drew his eyebrows together. "And when will you decide, huh?"

"Soon. Real soon. I'm making the final cuts this week."

"Cuts!" Zach didn't like the sound of the word. Hated it. It sounded so cold, so impersonal. This was his daughter they were talking about here. A little girl with feelings a yard wide, feelings one sharp word from Paige could decimate. And that, he wouldn't allow. "Jessie needs this, Paige. I told you I'd work with her. She can do it. I'll help her. Come on, show me the routine now."

How hard could the damn thing be to learn? This was a kiddie show, not a major stage production, for god's sake.

"I've been spending extra time with her, Zach. I'm sure she'll be ready."

"Show me the routine. I want to be *damned* sure."

"Zach, this is silly. I gave you my word."

He dragged her by the hand to the center of the room. "Come on, show me this fancy footwork."

The man could be unrelenting when it came to protecting his little girl. Paige wouldn't hurt Jessie for all the world. She wanted her to have her moment in the spotlight.

She would have Jessie ready for the recital, but Zach wasn't taking any chances.

"Okay, Zach," she said. "Let's see what you can do."

The guy would have all the innate grace of a wild armadillo, she was sure, but maybe if he knew the routine, he could run Jessie through it at home, Paige thought. Besides, seeing the big, sexy man trip across the floor in the *Dance of the Butterfly* or tap out *Twinkle Toes,* the tap number Jessie was working on, was an opportunity not to be missed.

Zach tried. Paige would have to give him credit for that. But her original prediction about his grace was highly overrated.

"I can do this," he said. "Just give me a break— okay?"

"I give you an *E* for effort. Now, let's try it again."

She patiently led him through a few of the simpler ballet steps, which he executed like a man in a suit of rusted armor.

"How'd I do?" he asked after a few more run-throughs. "I think I'm getting the hang of it."

Paige hadn't even shown him the routine to the Butterfly dance and already she knew this was an exercise in futility. "I think you better not quit your day job."

Zach deflated like a punctured tire. "Don't be so tough, lady. I'm not auditioning here—just trying to help my daughter."

"Yeah, well, maybe you'd be more help to Jessie if you didn't try."

"Are you gonna show me this dance or not?"

Not was the answer that came to mind, but she bit back the reply and took Zach under her wing—literally if not figuratively.

She used the hands-on approach.

She stood behind him, her body fit to his torso, her arms against his arms, her legs against his legs, so she could guide his movements, make him *feel* the grace of the motion. But *she* was the one who felt—and it wasn't grace. Just hard male muscle, firm buttocks, powerful legs and brawny shoulders. Her every nerve ending suddenly went on sensory alert.

Zach gave a low growl of approval. "Oh, babe—now this dance I can go for."

"This isn't a dance. It's just to show you how to move your body. And I'm not a babe!" It was better to focus on anger than the man she was trying to coach.

"Sorry," he said. "It's because I'm so close to all this rampant femininity."

Dealing with his rampant masculinity wasn't easy, either—but she didn't want to tell him that. Too late, she realized this had not been one of her better ideas. She didn't handle being in such proximity with Zach Delano well. She knew that.

So why was she closer than two peas in a pod with the man?

"Let's try it again," she said crisply. "Touch heels, toes apart. Keep your knees tight. Are they tight?"

"Yes. And I'm beginning to feel like a fool."

"Hey, this was your idea, big guy."

It was hard to keep her mind in a professional vein with a man so mind-blowingly male pressed up against her, but she was giving it her best effort. So was Zach, she realized. He would do just about anything for Jessie—even move his big body into unbendable positions.

"Slide your foot forward, toe pointed," she ordered. "Sliiiide." Paige tried to guide his right leg forward with her own behind it, but Zach chose to slide with his left, which sent them both off balance and brought him toppling down on top of her.

They landed in a heap on the floor, an intimate tangle of arms and legs. And hands in dangerous places, at least his hands, and they were . . . moving. The laughter that had been welling up in her stilled in her throat, and her breath caught.

"This dance I like even better," he purred close to her ear.

"Zach..."

"Hmm."

She wished his hands didn't feel so good, she wished his voice didn't sound so sexy against her ear, she wished his body didn't feel so virile pressed to hers as he held her. "This isn't a dance, either."

"Strange," he said, "I hear music." Then his mouth closed over hers.

Chapter Eight

This kiss was different. Paige knew it the moment his lips touched hers. Whatever had been going on between them from the start had escalated to something new, something frightening and powerful.

She trembled under his touch, the heat of his hands on her body. His mouth was sensual velvet and hard insistence as he demanded everything from her—her mind, her will, every helpless emotion. He teased and tortured her senses, her shaky sanity.

They wanted each other—and they were on a collision course with inevitability. If he asked her to at this moment, she would make love with him. Something that wasn't likely to happen with Jessie and the battleship Ernestine just a floor below. That should be reassuring to her, but somehow it wasn't.

She could feel the thudding of his heart against hers, her own matching it beat for frantic beat. A low moan tore from his throat, a raw, needy sound that echoed her own need. His weight pressed her to the floor, his body hard and heated as it covered hers.

"Paige..." Zach murmured her name, whispering it against the softness of her mouth. He wanted to soothe those pouty lips with the moistness of his tongue—but he didn't trust himself to do so. Paige was too overwhelming, too overpowering. "I didn't want this to happen between us," he said in a voice he barely recognized as his own.

She sighed, her breath warm and trembly. "I know. And I'm not sure what *is* happening, just that it's scary."

It was that. Zach kissed her quivering chin, then her creamy neck and dipped his tongue into the hollow of her throat, tasting the sweetness there. "So what do we do about it?" he asked. He buried his face in her hair that his frantic hands had loosened a few moments earlier.

He wanted to hear her answer, prayed it was one that would send him away from her, prayed it was one that wouldn't.

"Nothing—we do nothing," she said, sounding all too much like the voice of cool logic, something he was far from possessing at the moment.

A sigh shuddered out of him. "Nothing?"

"Yes." It had to be this way, Paige knew, or she would lose herself in him.

From somewhere in the lower region of the house, Jessie's childish laughter streamed upward, soft and sweet and distant. But it was a reminder to Paige of how tightly Zach held on to those he loved. Even this room she gazed up at from her spot beneath him on the floor was evidence of just how much he could coddle and pamper and take care of every aspect of someone's life. Jessie's.

And if Paige gave in, let things run their inevitable course, *let herself love this man*, he would do the same to her. She knew she didn't dare let him into her life, any more than she already had. Yet, could she possibly keep him out when her heart desperately wanted him there?

"I'm not sure 'nothing' is an option," he whispered with a withdrawing nip to her lower lip. "But for now it'll have to be."

Paige knew things weren't settled between them, only put on hold temporarily. Jessie would be back up here at any moment—or Ernestine. They were her safety net this time, but what about next time?

Paige could barely drive home, Zach had her so shaken.

Jessie had begged her to stay for dinner and strawberry shortcake, but Paige had offered an excuse—and Zach had allowed her to. He'd known she was as unnerved as he by what had happened between them, what would have happened had they been alone—without Jessie and Ernestine nearby. They would have made love, wild and helpless love, denying each other nothing.

A thrill ran through her at the thought of Zach's heated body pressed to hers, hard and sleek and male. She knew he would be a passionate lover, taking her to peaks she'd never imagined.

She gave a shuddery sigh, then realized she'd just passed her street. She offered a colorful curse and circled the block.

What was Zach doing to her? She was finally living life on her own. She was happy and content running DanceWorks. It was her dream realized. In a few weeks she'd be putting on her very first recital.

The real Paige had at long last emerged from her cocoon, a new butterfly, unsteady, but with a determined will to fly. She knew who she was, what she wanted to accomplish. Zach could only complicate her life, this life she'd struggled to mold for herself. Alone and on her own—that was the way she wanted things.

Reaching her driveway, she pulled in and parked her car in front of the garage, leaving it outside because the single-car space was filled with the scenery props she had to finish painting. Tonight she would busy herself doing just that. She'd absorb herself in her work and dream of how each backdrop would look on opening night, her little munchkins trouping across the lighted stage in front of them.

Yes, that was what she would do, and maybe—just maybe—she could forget the sweet, hot passion of Zach's lips.

* * *

"How's the recital shaping up? Need any help? I've got two big, strong shoulders." Zach couldn't refrain from calling and offering.

Again.

He knew Paige wanted autonomous control of the production, or at least she didn't want *him* butting in, but he couldn't help himself. It had been three whole days since he'd seen her, three days since they'd shared that kiss, knocking him into the next county.

She was busy, very busy. With the recital looming on the horizon she and Ernestine had been totally engrossed in getting the costumes ready. And he'd gotten short shrift in the attention department.

Even Jessie hadn't had time for her dad. All she could bubble about was the dance number she was going to have in the recital and the pretty tutu Ernestine would be making for her as soon as the fabric arrived. When she wasn't talking about the upcoming show, she was practicing for it.

Zach's own attempts in that regard had been a failure—except for that warm thrill he got whenever he thought about the intimate little tumble he and Paige had landed in. And he thought about it a lot—the heat of her supple body beneath his, the devastating softness of her lips and the passion he'd tasted on them.

"Zach, everything's under control," Paige returned, her voice sounding so far away. He'd rather hear it close to his ear, calling out his name when he made love to her.

"What do you mean, under control?" He knew it couldn't be. She had a million details she was dealing with. Alone. When he could be helping out.

She'd stayed up until three in the morning painting scenery props the other night, he'd learned from Ernestine. And she'd lost her one and only stagehand. The guy had fallen from a ladder and broken his wrist while painting his house, which left Paige with no one for the job—except, of course, himself. But when he'd offered his services, Paige had turned him down flat, saying she would find someone.

"Just that," she replied. "Everything's going fine."

He hated the sound of that proud defiance he heard in her. He understood where it came from, understood the number her ex-husband had done on her, but he still didn't like it. He didn't like her taking on the whole shebang alone when he was perfectly capable of giving her a hand.

"Define 'everything.' Ernie says you're doing too much and losing sleep."

"Well, Ernie talks too much. I'm doing okay, Zach—really. But thank you for worrying about me."

Paige sighed, hating the fact that it felt good to have this man concerned about her. It would be so good to give in to his offers to help, so easy to slide into his arms and take all the warm comfort he could give her, let him kiss away the doubts she had about herself, her fears about her first big show, but she couldn't. That would be a giant step backward.

She had to prove Paige Hanford could do this on her own. She had to prove Stephen wrong, prove she was more than capable of achieving her own successes in this world.

"At least take a break and relax long enough to have pizza with Jessie and me after her lesson tonight. How about it?"

"Oh, Zach, it's tempting, but I can't. I have so much I need to do." She would love nothing better than to spend an evening with Zach and Jessie, an evening to talk about nothing, to laugh, to let down and relax.

On the other hand, she felt guilty about every moment she didn't spend working on the recital. The details seemed endless. She'd scratch one item from her checklist only to replace it with two more she hadn't thought about—and that was on a good day.

"Paige, whatever you have to do can wait. Either that, or I'll stay and help you—*then* we'll go for pizza," Zach proposed in no uncertain terms, and Paige knew she was caught. One way or another, she would have his company.

And pizza was the lesser of the two evils, she decided. If Zach stayed to give her a hand, he'd soon be taking over. "Okay, Zach, after Jessie's lesson we'll go for a *quick* pizza." She stressed the quick, and it was a vow she intended to keep—no matter how good a time she was having with them.

A few hours later, Zach arrived with Jessie in tow for her ballet session. He sat in on the lesson, taking up a position on Paige's piano bench. Paige was prepared to shoo him out if he so much as sneezed to distract them, but surprisingly he behaved. He stayed out of their way and remained silent, watching Jessie's attempts with a smile on his face and an adoring look in his silver-gray eyes. Occasionally his gaze strayed to Paige, lingering on her lazily, but instead of being annoyed by it, she felt all warm inside.

Once, he wandered out to the garage to inspect her handiwork on the scenery props. He returned with words of praise for her talent, and Paige tucked the compliment next to her heart. Stephen would have had a criticism to pass along, something snide or belittling. The pain of the past had wounded her deeply. What Stephen had done had left its mark on her.

And perhaps—just perhaps—she'd been judging Zach by that past hurt.

She thought about it as she and Zach and Jessie shared their pizza. She tried to look at Zach through new eyes, more open eyes. Tonight he'd been the epitome of good grace. He'd allowed Paige to do the teaching, while he remained the dutiful observer. Was he trying to turn over a new leaf?

His gaze hadn't strayed once to Jessie as she enjoyed the play area while he and Paige lingered over cold drinks. He loved his daughter, and she would always be his precious little girl, but perhaps he was softening his vigilance of her. Just a little.

"Sorry you came tonight?" he asked, drawing her back from her thoughts. He reached for her hand,

folding it in his, which made Paige feel safe and secure.

It was a feeling she hadn't allowed herself lately, and
maybe she shouldn't now. But Zach's touch was
tempting. So was the man. Very. "I'm enjoying the
company—even if I should be home doing other
things."

Tonight she didn't want to think about the recital.
She wanted to smile at Zach across the table, watch
Jessie play nearby and bask in the feeling that she be-
longed here. With them.

"Good, then Ernie won't have to worry about
you," he quipped.

She gave him a suspicious glance. "I think you're
the one doing all the worrying."

"Do you mind?"

He stroked her palm lightly and sensations rico-
cheted through her like skyrockets. "I'm a big girl
now. I don't need anyone to take care of me, thank
you."

But how easy it would be to allow this man to do so,
she thought. How easy to let him love her. His face
looked lean and handsome in the soft lighting, his jaw
square and determined, with just a hint of an evening
beard shadowing it.

He had on the same forest-green sweater he'd been
wearing the day she'd met with him in the park. It
stretched across his hard muscles, inviting hands to
touch.

His eyes were dark and observant, not missing a nuance of an expression on her face as she scrutinized his body. Turnabout was only fair play, she thought, as she remembered his gaze on her at times during the evening.

"I haven't forgotten you're a big girl, believe me," he said, his voice low, rumbly. He held her hand prisoner in his, the flat of his thumb caressing her palm with erotic thoroughness.

She couldn't move, couldn't draw away. She could barely think. His eyes slid over her face, then softened on her mouth. Paige could feel the heat of it. She wanted him to kiss her, dangerous as she knew that would be. "Zach..."

She had to tell him to stop. She had to tell him her emotions were on a very short fuse—and she wasn't sure she could resist him tonight, *any* night, but words wouldn't come.

"Do you know what you do to me, woman?" he said with a low groan.

Paige's mind flashed back to the other afternoon, their dance lesson that had gone awry. Yes, she knew. "Zach, this...this isn't what either of us needs in our life right now."

"Needs is what all this is about, I'm afraid. Yours and mine. This may not be something we need in our life—but it's there just the same."

It was there and it wasn't going away, Paige knew. "Zach..."

"I know you're not ready, Paige. I'm not, either, not for anything serious. And you're a serious kind of woman, the kind I'd promised myself I'd stay away from. I . . . I just thought you should know my reasons for wanting, *needing,* to see you are not totally honorable."

And she wanted Zach, too, knowing he could be nothing casual to her, knowing he was all wrong for her. She'd come through something painful in her life, with everything bruised except her hormones, it seemed.

Zach had been through pain, too. And there was nothing wrong with his set of hormones. She only hoped he could hold on to that honor of his because she wasn't sure how long she could resist him.

"Forewarned is forearmed?" she asked with more levity than she felt.

"Something like that . . ."

Just then Paige caught a glimpse of Jessie racing toward them, her glasses atilt on her small face, as usual, and her cheeks flushed from play. "Did you see me, Miss Paige? Did you see me on the big slide?"

Paige had seen little else but Zach, but she couldn't tell Jessie that. "Yes, I, uh, sure did, sweetheart. Are you having a good time?"

"Uh-huh."

She pulled Jessie close, holding on to her as if she were a lifeline, a chaperon for her dangerous feelings.

Over the next few weeks, Zach was ever present in

Paige's life. He brought Jessie to her lessons, he called every day to see how Paige was, if she needed his help, if she was working too hard. Each time, she refused the help he offered, but a part of her, a secret part, a *weak* part, wanted to accept it, wanted him there in her life.

She stayed busy, too busy to think about the devastation of his smile, how good his arms felt around her, how much she wanted him.

The recital was looming—only weeks away. Ernestine had the costumes almost completed, including two for Jessie, a soft yellow tutu for her butterfly ballet number and a bright pink satin for her tap number. Jessie would be the one on the end, tapping slightly out of rhythm. The image brought a slow smile to Paige's lips. Jessie was Jessie, a little girl with two left feet and miles of spirit. And it was that spirit that would endear her to the audience, Paige knew.

"Did you find that new stagehand yet?" Ernestine asked when Paige dropped off more sequins and thread one afternoon.

She'd come at this time of day, knowing Zach would be in court and she wouldn't likely run into him. "No, Ernie, not anyone experienced—or even inexperienced. What's worse, my lighting director just quit. He got a better offer in Kansas City, a *professional* production." Which hers was not.

Ernestine picked through the tiny bags of sequins Paige had brought and plucked out a package of silver ones to sew on the midnight-blue taffeta she was working with. "Well, I have a solution to your stage-hand problem," she said with a quirk of a smile.

"You have?" Paige's answer was excitement mixed with a hint of wariness.

"I sure do. And if you talk real sweet to him, he just might give you a hand with the lighting, too."

"Who, Ernie?" Paige suspected she knew who the housekeeper had in mind for the job and she didn't like it one bit.

"You won't get a better offer. Or a cheaper one," Ernestine advised her. "He's willing to work for free."

"Zach," Paige said, assured she was right. "I don't know, Ernie. I don't know about this."

She rubbed her temples, feeling the beginning of a headache, not the first one she'd had over the show that just might go on with her as its only backstage worker—except for a sound man she wasn't sure was qualified. The fellow was so elderly and doddery, he was probably tone-deaf.

"Well, of course, this is your recital. You can keep on looking for someone and hope you find them," the woman said with all-knowing wiseness, "or you can let Zach help out."

Paige sighed. She knew she would have to give in and accept Zach's generosity and cling to the faint hope he wouldn't ride roughshod over her production.

Or her life.

"Okay, Ernie," she said bleakly. "Tell him he has the job if he wants it."

She could always fire him if someone better came along. Or if his take-charge attitude got in the way.

Zach walked around the empty theater with Paige, trying to see the old barn of a place through her eyes. She saw it filled with an excited audience, the house-lights dimmed, the stage bright with her hopeful young dancers. He also knew she saw more, she saw success and her own personal accomplishment.

He wanted her to have the accomplishment that was so important to her—and he would do what he could to see that she got it.

"Any questions?" she asked when she'd finished explaining his backstage duties.

"Just one," he said.

"What's that?"

He brushed a wispy curl away from her flushed cheek. "When are you going to ease up on yourself? You've thought of everything. This show could run itself, so why don't you just relax and enjoy it?"

She narrowed her eyes at him. He could see their sassy green color in the dim light of the dusty old theater. "Shows what you know, Zach Delano. I still have a million things to do and I'm not leaving *anything* to chance. As for enjoying myself, I'll do that after the final curtain."

"I see." He drew his hand away and folded his arms across his chest to keep from touching her again. Touching her was all he thought about lately—and making love to her. No woman had ever affected him like Paige had. One small half-pint of a woman had brought him down, but good. And he didn't know what he was going to do about it.

Maybe it was time to trust again, trust in the magic of love that he'd denied for so long. He didn't know. Paige had come into his and Jessie's life—and into their hearts.

She made her way toward the exit with its faint red light over the double doors. He followed behind, trying to keep his gaze off her sexy wiggle.

"At least come to dinner tonight," he proposed. "By then I may have a few more questions about these stage duties of mine."

She turned and eyed him warily.

"*Please...*" He wasn't above begging if it meant he could smile across the table at her. Besides, he wanted to see if she looked as if she belonged there, in that place across from him, a part of his little family.

He suspected she would.

"Zach, I . . ." She paused. "Well, I do have to drop off some fabric for Ernie, some tulle she needs so she can finish up the last of the costumes," she said. "And I do need to talk to you about my sound man."

"Oh? A problem?"

"I don't know yet."

Zach hadn't wanted business to be her reason for coming, but then the show was her whole life right now—and that was something he would have to understand. "Dinner's at six-thirty," he said. "Too early?"

She checked her watch. "No—I can make that."

He resisted leaning down to kiss her, knowing he wouldn't be able to stop with just one. Instead, he shoved open the double door for her, giving a sigh of regret as she walked out into the fading afternoon sunlight.

Yes, he'd have to think about this love thing.

Paige drove away from the theater, feeling oddly disconcerted. She was certain Zach had been about to kiss her, but the moment had passed, unacted upon. She couldn't deny she'd been waiting for the kiss, like a parched flower waiting for a morning rain shower.

Zach was a distraction she didn't need in her life right now. The recital was less than two weeks away. Countdown time. And she needed to keep her scattered wits about her.

All in all, the afternoon had gone well. Zach had shown a quick grasp of what she expected him to handle backstage on her most important night. He'd offered his own opinion a time or two, but in the end, deferred to her judgment.

If she was lucky, real lucky, maybe she could get through this without his calling all the shots. One fact remained, she needed him backstage. . . .

And just maybe in her life.

She'd gotten about four blocks from the theater when she remembered she had meant to check out the condition of the speakers. The building was old, its sound equipment ancient, maybe as ancient as the sound technician she'd hired on. She couldn't trust that the man would hear a screech emanating from a high speaker at some shining moment in the show.

She glanced at her watch. If she hurried, she had just enough time to go back and still make it to Zach's without being late for dinner.

The extra key the custodian had given her fit the stage door only. She let herself in and fumbled for a light switch, unsure in the dark and gloom just where it was located.

The theater wasn't used much, only for an occasional summer play when a road troupe was passing through town. Most performers preferred to go to Kansas City, where the audiences were larger.

Paige had never danced here. She'd known the backstage of the former Majestic down to the last board and footlight, but after a few rehearsals, this place would begin to seem like home, she knew.

She found the switch and flipped it on. Welcoming light flooded the room. At the same moment, her foot sank into an old board, rotten with age, sending her sprawling.

Pain seared through her right leg, pain so fierce, so intense she had to have shattered the bone. The room swirled and dark spots flickered in front of her eyes. She fought for consciousness, but she could feel the blackness swallow her.

Chapter Nine

Zach tried not to show his rising panic in front of Jessie. Paige was late, very late. His gut clenched with the fear that something was wrong.

He'd called her house, hoping to hear the sweet sound of her voice, hoping she'd only become preoccupied with some detail of the recital and forgotten the time, but there was no answer. No answer at all.

"I don't think I can hold up this dinner much longer," Ernestine said, her words intruding into his increasingly blacker thoughts. "The little miss is getting hungry."

He stared at the housekeeper blankly for a brief moment, then forced reason to return at least temporarily. "Go ahead and let Jessie eat," he said. "And yourself, Ernie. I'll wait until Paige gets here. Something...something has just held her up, I'm sure."

Ernestine nodded. She didn't buy his attempt at casualness, he knew. He saw it in her face, but she didn't offer a comment, only grasped Jessie's hand and led her toward the kitchen, promising her that she could have ice cream with the grown-ups later...when Miss Paige arrived.

Jessie accepted this and tripped along merrily beside Ernestine. Zach returned to his pacing. If anything had happened to Paige...

He tried to ignore the gnawing fear that there'd been an accident, the terror that history could repeat itself. No...fate could not be that cruel, not a second time. Paige was all right, she had to be all right.

At this moment, she was probably buying a bouquet of flowers for tonight's dinner table, not even realizing she was late. His mind focused on that, instead of the other horror—that she might be hurt, that she might be needing him and he wasn't there for her.

Like another night when he hadn't been there for the woman he loved.

The woman he loved—

He did love Paige. He could no longer deny it. And by some cruel twist, he knew he had to stop loving her.

It would only bring him pain, like the pain of the past, the pain he thought he was finally getting beyond. And the fear he thought he'd been putting behind him as well. The fear that harm might somehow come to Jessie, that he would fail her the way he'd failed Janet. He couldn't live with the fear that he might fail Paige, too.

He paced to the window, parted the slats of the front blinds and peered out into the dark night, but no car crept down the quiet street. He let the blinds snap back into place. He'd seen Paige a little more than an hour ago, he reasoned, her green eyes bright, sassy. Her lips soft and tempting. She'd been fine then. What could happen in that short a time?

That thought sent ice rushing through his veins. He knew too well that tragedy took only seconds, one second, a half second.

He strode to the phone and jerked up the receiver, dialing a friend he knew on the police force. Ben would tell him if there were any accidents working. Why hadn't he thought of it sooner?

"Ben? Zach," he said when his friend picked up on the third ring. "Do me a favor and see if there've been any vehiculars reported in the past hour." He rubbed the back of his neck at Ben's need to know the reason for his query. "Just do it, Ben. I'll explain later."

It took Ben what seemed like forever to check and report back.

"Nothing? Not a one?" Zach questioned tersely.

His friend assured him that was right.

"Thanks, Ben. I owe you one," he said, then hung up.

Frustration settled in. Maybe he should try the

hospital.... But before he could reach for the phone again, it rang. His hand hesitated an inch above the receiver, then he snatched it up, snapping a brusque hello.

"Zach..."

"Paige?" Her voice sounded so far away. He wanted to reach through the phone line and hug her to him. "What is it? Where are you?"

"At the hospital...the emergency room. I'm sorry about dinner, but I had a little mishap. My leg—"

Zach's breath caught in his throat and his stomach lurched. Paige was at the hospital. She needed him. "I'm on my way," he said without a moment's hesitation.

He shouted to Ernestine that he had to go out, then raced to the Bronco before she or Jessie could ask questions.

The hospital was less than a mile away, but it might as well have been on the other side of the earth. He pressed the accelerator, urging the car faster, as fast as he dared in the late-evening traffic. Why hadn't he asked what had happened? If she was all right? But he knew words wouldn't reassure him. Only seeing Paige could do that, feeling her whole and safe in his arms.

Her leg... That could mean anything. His mind didn't want to consider the possibilities. If Paige couldn't dance... The school was her life. Dance defined who she was at a time when she needed that definition. The recital she'd put all her heart and soul into was coming together. It was the ruby in her crown of independence. But she also wanted it for the kids, her pupils, her shining stars.

Zach reached the hospital in harrowing record time, parked and raced toward the entrance. Just inside, he hesitated as the sights and smells assailed his senses, the same sights and smells he remembered from a long-ago night. The town, the hospital, were different—yet not so different. He reached for the wall, planting a broad hand against it as images swept through his memory bank, memories that returned in cruel déjà vu, memories he knew he could never erase. Tonight, when Paige hadn't arrived, they'd begun trickling back. Now they returned in all their horrifying clarity.

Janet . . . His precious Jessie . . . His own feelings of inadequacy and helplessness that night.

Only Jessie had pulled through. Jessie, who had clung to his neck and refused to let go. And he'd refused to let her go—as he'd had to do with Janet.

"Are you all right, sir?" A nurse passing by placed a cool hand on his arm.

He swallowed tightly and shrugged off her touch. "I'm fine," he growled, not wanting her—anyone—to hear the sound of his emotions fragmenting. "Just tell me which way to the emergency room."

Paige tried to shift her body on the narrow ER cart, the pain in her now trussed-up right leg ebbing with the effects of the medication.

The custodian had found her, administered rudimentary first aid and brought her here. Only after being assured Zach was on his way had he left her—with an apology and an avowal to check every last board and shore up the old flooring before her big night.

At least there would be a big night.

Miraculously there'd been no fracture, only a bad wrench to her ankle and one jagged laceration, which the doctor had quickly sutured. She wriggled her toes poking out from the huge wrapping—just to reassure herself they all worked. They did.

She wished she could have reassured Zach that she was all right, but he'd hung up before giving her a chance.

She shoved herself to a sitting position and glanced around the small, sterile cubicle. Her nose wrinkled at the smell of antiseptic that seemed to permeate everything. The medication was making her a little fuzzy headed and she didn't like the feeling that she wasn't in control. Maybe because it reminded her she wasn't in control of her life as well right now. Zach had her in a turmoil.

Her last thought before she'd passed out from the pain had been of him. That she loved him. Loved him without rhyme or reason. Without common sense.

But then, love wasn't supposed to be inspected too closely.

Love was just there.

She heard his voice asking for her a moment before he stepped inside the curtain. Her first impulse was one of relief that he was here, he would kiss her and make her life glow again, but that was quickly negated by the pallor she saw on his face.

The pallor frightened her.

So did the way he held her—as if she would break in two. Or evaporate into thin air. "Zach, I—I'm fine. I'm really fine. It's just a silly old wrenched ankle."

He touched her face, then her lips with trembly fingers, finally brushing a hand over the wrapping on her foot. "Are you sure? I mean, the bandage..."

"There was a cut, too, but the doctor stitched me up." She wiggled her toes as proof she was in one piece, that he didn't have to look so glum. "It's just that they wouldn't let me go home unless I was with someone, and I didn't want Duncan to take me, so I called—"

"Who's Duncan?" he interrupted what must have sounded like delirious rambling—and maybe it was. The shot they'd given her had packed a wallop.

"Duncan's the man who found me—the man who looks after the theater."

"What were you doing at the theater? I thought we were finished there."

"We were. I mean, you and I were. But then I thought of something I needed to check, so I went back and fell through this old board in the floor."

She waited for him to tell her what a dumb thing she'd done, that she was foolish and silly for getting hurt, the way Stephen would have, making her feel it had all somehow been her fault, but Zach didn't. He stroked her cheek, the pallor that had begun to fade from his face returning.

"Zach . . . I'm fine."

He slammed a fist against the cart. "Damn it, Paige, you could have been hurt. Seriously hurt. Why hadn't someone checked out that floor?"

"Zach, the building's old. It happens. Duncan's going to see that it doesn't again."

"But your leg could have been shattered."

She sobered quickly and studied her fingernails. Her voice was low. "I know." Then her smile brightened. "But it wasn't. I was lucky."

"Luck is not a secure commodity. Luck . . . doesn't keep someone safe." The anger in him had turned to quiet rage. Rage turned inward. At something that couldn't be controlled. By him.

Was he thinking of Janet? The accident that had changed his and Jessie's life so quickly? So irrevocably? Her gaze swept over his face, the worry lines that seemed deeper tonight, and she knew the answer.

"Zach . . ." She reached out to touch him, soothe away the past, but he caught her hand and drew it away.

"Come on, let's get you out of here," he said brusquely.

The nurse fitted her with a pair of crutches she was to use for the next few days and gave her a small packet of pain pills, should she need them, then released her to Zach's care.

Zach was silent on the way to Paige's house. Tonight had brought his old fears to the forefront of his
mind and he didn't know how to tell Paige that, didn't
know how to make her understand that no matter how
much he loved her, no matter how special she was to
him, he had to back away from what he wanted
most—her fragile, soft body in his arms forever.

The fear of losing her would just be too great.

He would smother her, trying to keep her safe, protected. And Paige would hate him for it, would hate
the prison he would put her in.

He glanced over at her, looking so beautiful in the
pale light. He should never have fallen in love with her.
Love only brought pain to all who got caught up in it.
How could he have forgotten that?

Now he'd hurt Paige, he'd hurt himself. And Jessie. His daughter would be hurt, too, and he hated
that.

When they'd reached her house, Zach helped Paige
down out of the Bronco, but in her fierce independence, she insisted on walking to the door under her
own steam. "In a few days, I intend to be dancing
again," she said.

He looked her up and down, then gave her a serious frown. "I don't doubt that you'll try even sooner,
but tonight you are going to rest that ankle like the
doctor said."

"I am?"

A smile edged at her lips, a smile he wanted to taste.
"You are," he returned, managing to hold firm.

Once inside, he snatched up a couple of the toss pillows decorating the floor in her furniture-less living room, strode to that pretty apricot and green bedroom of hers and plopped them at the end of her bed. Then he plumped two bed pillows to put at her back.

"Get horizontal," he told her, "while I fix you a bite to eat. You missed dinner, as I recall."

She turned serious. "Zach, you don't have to take care of me. I'm—"

"I know—a big girl." He took in every inch of her, then sucked in a breath, remembering he was here to make her comfortable, nothing else.

"Really, Zach, I don't want anything to eat. If I get hungry later—"

"You'll hobble around in the kitchen on a pair of crutches when you shouldn't. Now, unless you need help getting out of those clothes, I'm going out there and find you some nourishment."

She sank onto the bed with a sigh and kicked off her shoe. The other was still at the theater, caught in one jagged piece of flooring, he suspected. A knot of anger rose up in him all over again. A helpless, frustrated anger.

He turned and headed toward the kitchen.

"Now, that's more like it," he said when he returned a few moments later with a glass of cold milk and an omelet he'd quickly whipped together and found her following orders. What he didn't understand was how someone could look so incredibly sexy in a soft-washed, high-necked nightgown, but Paige had managed to accomplish the feat in spades.

She'd loosened her long braid and the strands spilled across the pillows at her back. He wanted to feel her hair against his palm, whisper through his fingers, smell its fragrance, but he'd declared Paige off-limits.

Still, her body tempted him, the shape of her rounded breasts softly defined against the fabric of her gown, her waist his hands could span, the gentle curve of her hips. She'd propped her leg on the bank of pillows at the end of the bed, her toes peeking out from the wrapping.

"I hope you like omelets," he said, "because that's my specialty, my *only* specialty."

Paige could think of one other—the way the man kissed. And her healthy imagination could supply yet another. "I doubt that, Zach Delano," she said. And upon seeing the flash of awareness in his eyes, she regretted her words.

He didn't smile. Instead, a muscle worked along his jawline. He was fighting against something—and she instinctively knew it was *her*.

She affected him more than he wanted to be affected.

Something had happened between them, something frightening. Zach had been quiet, *too* quiet, on the drive home, and Paige didn't think it was all worry over her injury. He could see she was fine, a little hobbled temporarily, but nothing more.

She thought she knew what frightened him, but she wanted to hear him say it. No matter the consequences, she had to know the extent of the battle she was up against.

She put down her fork. "What is it, Zach? Something's wrong, and I think we need to talk about it."

His gaze stroked her face for a long moment, and she'd never seen eyes so troubled, so much in pain. Then he gave her a faint half smile. "You need that omelet. And the milk—milk builds strong bones," he said, his voice husky-harsh. "Then a good night's sleep."

He fought another internal war with himself, then leaned down and kissed her, a soft brush across her mouth, a kiss that tasted like regret.

Then he turned and left.

Bright and early the next morning, Ernestine was at her door. Beside her stood Jessie, carrying flowers and looking so forlorn Paige wanted to hug the little girl.

"We came to check on you," Ernestine said, her voice gruff to hide her kind deed.

"Uh-huh, and I brought you these," Jessie added solemnly, presenting her with the flowers she clutched in her little hand.

Paige's eyes misted. She'd never had a sweeter gift or one that meant so much. "They're so pretty, Jessie," she said, giving them a sniff. "And thank you for coming, Ernie."

The older woman sighed with a snort of indifference, but it didn't fool Paige.

"Come in, and we'll put these in water."

"Where are your crutches? My daddy said you got crutches," Jessie said.

Paige gave her a smile. "Well, don't tell your daddy, but right now they're propping up the wall in my kitchen."

Jessie giggled, and Ernestine clucked her tongue and rolled her eyes.

Paige began to feel better. Last night after Zach had left, she felt as if the world had come to an end. At least *her* world. But now she knew one small corner of it was bright and wonderful.

She hobbled her way toward the kitchen and let Jessie help her fill a vase with water, then they arranged the flowers in it and placed it in the middle of the kitchen table. Paige put on some coffee for herself and Ernestine and fixed Jessie a glass of fresh-squeezed orange juice.

Paige and Ernestine discussed a few details of the recital, enjoying the coffee. Jessie drank her juice beside them, perched on the chair, one of her little legs swinging to and fro in no apparent rhythm.

"Can I walk with your crutches?" Jessie asked after a moment. "I never had crutches before."

"And I hope you never have to have them, sweetheart."

"So can I, please?"

Paige mentally measured the crutches she'd parked against the wall early this morning, declaring them more of a handicap than her injured ankle, then gauged Jessie's size. "I think they're a little too tall for you, but you can try them out if you like."

"Yea!"

Jessie stumped around the kitchen in them, the tops sticking out from behind her arms. "My daddy was real worried about you," she said as she hopped about. "I could tell."

Paige's eyelids flickered, but other than that, she gave away little of the emotion churning inside her. "Oh? And . . . and how could you tell that?"

Jessie crossed the kitchen floor again. "'Cause he cut himself shaving, then said a naughty word that Ernestine makes him put a whole quarter in the jar for."

Paige hid a grin.

"Then he poured orange juice over his cereal instead of milk. He said another naughty word, and dumped his bowl in the sink, and then he said he wasn't hungry and went to work. Then we came here," she finished.

"And I'm so glad you did."

Paige was also glad to know she could manage to upset the man enough he had to put money in Ernestine's swear jar. She wished it was lots of quarters—until he was so upset he would talk to her about what was bothering him, so they could try to work it out.

She could hope. At least she'd be seeing him again—unless he intended to resign as her stagehand.

Paige stepped inside the old theater building and found new boards interspersed among the old. In some places there were whole new sections of flooring, then it had been mopped and cleaned until it shone.

"Duncan, are you here?" Paige called out to the custodian. When she received no answer, she called again.

After a moment, he appeared, loping easily toward her. "Miss Hanford, you're in one piece again."

Paige smiled. It had been a week since her mishap. Her right leg still sported a small ankle brace, but the stitches were out and she'd returned the crutches to the hospital for someone who *really* needed them. "Of course I am. I have a show to put on. And the new floor is . . . is . . . Duncan, how did you do all this?"

"You like it?" Duncan scratched his slightly balding pate, looking pleased, more than pleased.

"Very much. How on earth did you get it done so quickly?"

"Well, I had a little help in that department. Actually, quite a lot of help. From a nice fellow who said he's your . . . stagehand."

Her eyes widened in surprise. "Zach? Zach helped you?"

"That he did. Went over the place with a fine-tooth comb, insisting every board that barely squeaked be fixed or replaced. Worked here till late every night."

Paige swallowed a lump that had climbed up in her throat. She hadn't seen Zach all week, not since the night he'd brought her home from the hospital and tucked her in bed.

He'd called a few times to check on her, to see if she was following doctor's orders—and she'd told him what he wanted to hear. Yes, she was following orders. And she had been—at least when it was convenient. But he hadn't brought Jessie to her lesson, hadn't stopped by to see her.

Paige knew they needed to talk, but she'd been so busy, both with the recital and her classes, that no opportunity had presented itself.

Now she knew what Zach had been doing with his evenings. Every evening—until late at night. Whether he wanted to admit it or not, he cared about her— enough to see that she was safe and that her little dance troupe wouldn't have any misadventures on opening night.

"Thank you, Duncan, for telling me that. And thank you for all the work you've done." She intended to thank Zach, too.

Whether he wanted her to or not.

She didn't know if things could be worked out between them. Maybe the past had too great a hold on him. Maybe they were both victims of their pasts, too much so for them to ever connect.

All she knew was that she had to find out.

"See me, Daddy? See me? I'm a pretty dancer."

Jessie pranced and pirouetted in front of him in the pale yellow tutu that Ernestine had just finished sewing for her.

"You sure are, honey—the prettiest," he said, a slow smile curving his lips.

She ruffled the tulle skirt with her hands, watching it spring back in its stiffness. "I like this one better than the pink one," she said as she danced across the living-room floor.

He grinned. Last week she'd thought the pink satin was the most beautiful costume there could ever be. He was grateful Paige had put Jessie in two numbers. It meant everything to his little girl, but then he thought Paige knew that.

Paige. It had been hell keeping his distance from her this past week. Worse than hell. Right now he wished he hadn't been so eager to volunteer his help backstage. It would mean seeing her more often during these last few days before her revue, as the show all came together. And his life came apart.

Just then, Ernestine appeared in the doorway, ready to see her small charge off to bed. The tender tyrant loved Jessie as much as he did, he knew. And the three of them were a family of sorts. He tamped down the thought that Paige could make them a real family, that she could add the love that would bind them together, make their happiness complete.

But happiness wasn't a given in life; he'd forgotten that briefly.

"Young miss, I want you upstairs, out of that costume and ready for bed in three minutes," Ernestine barked. She turned to Zach. "She had to show her daddy," she explained.

"It's okay, Ernie."

He knew the two of them had been walking on eggshells around him this week because he'd been uncharacteristically irritable. Not that he'd been home much. He'd had more than his share of court cases this week; then he'd spent his nights at that barn of a theater seeing what he and the custodian of the place could do with the old flooring. He didn't want another accident like the one that Paige had had. Not to Paige, not to anyone, for that matter.

"Jessie, do what Ernie says," Zach told her gently.

Her lower lip puckered, which always hit him in the gut and made him want to back down—every time. "Do I hafta go to bed? I want to practice."

"Practice is good, but so is sleep. Dancers need sleep if they want to perform well," he said with the quickest bribe that came to mind.

She shoved her small glasses up on her nose. "Okay," she relented, then flung her arms around his neck to give him a kiss. "Will you come and tuck me in?" she asked.

"I sure will, sweetheart." It was his favorite time of day.

After giving Jessie five minutes' head start, he put down the brief he'd been reading for court next week and went upstairs to her room. She looked so small and innocent, propped against her pillows, her latest favorite book on her lap.

She handed him the book open to the story she wanted him to read to her. He smiled, hating the time when she'd outgrow this nightly ritual, hating the time when she'd begin to date, presenting him with a whole host of new worries to deal with.

Could he ever keep her totally safe from harm? Was Paige right, did he need to release his tight hold on his daughter?

Then he thought of the blow life had dealt him, that life had dealt Jessie, and he knew he couldn't relax his vigilance—he didn't dare.

After only ten minutes of reading, Jessie was off in slumberland, no doubt dreaming of butterfly dances and other things her little world was currently filled with. He only wished his own dreams could be as untroubled.

He kissed Jessie lightly on the forehead and crept quietly back downstairs to fix himself a brandy—and ponder how he'd ever be able to make life go on without Paige in it.

He was on his second drink, with no answer arrived at, when he heard the front doorbell. He knew Ernestine had retired for the night, so he went to the door himself.

Paige stood there on the other side, looking like something he might have conjured up out of his dreams. He'd never seen her look more beautiful, more tempting, than she did at that moment. He'd never felt more ill equipped to resist her sweetness.

Her hair spilled over her shoulders in tawny splendor, neither blond nor brown, but a glorious celebration of both. She was dressed in blue jeans that cupped her every feminine curve and a pale green V-neck pullover. In the deep V was a hint of delicate lace. From a camisole? he wondered. His hands itched to discover if it was, his body jealous of the small scrap of cloth pressed to that delectable part of her.

He swallowed hard. "This is a surprise," he said. "Come in."

"Thank you."

She stepped inside, and Zach hated the formality that seemed to surround them. He wanted to haul her into his arms and never let her go. He wanted to kiss her, caress her, make her his forever.

He drew a shaky breath. "I was just having a brandy. Care for one?"

Her eyes widened at him as she studied his face, then she glanced at the glass he held in his hand. "Yes, that might be nice."

He led her into the living room and poured her a brandy he'd retrieved from the small cabinet over the glassed-in bookcases.

"What brings you out? I'd have thought you'd be knee-deep in recital preparations," he said, handing her the small brandy snifter.

Their fingers brushed and, as usual, it felt as though he'd been caught in an electrical storm. He quickly withdrew his hand and took a step away from her. For peace of mind as well as necessity.

"I thought we should talk," she said.

"Talk? About what?"

She took a seat at one end of the sofa, tried a small sip of brandy, her pretty hands curved around the bowl of the glass. "Several things. The first of which is a thank-you, a great big thank-you, for helping Duncan fix the flooring." She looked up at him from over her glass. "But I have the feeling Duncan was helping *you,* instead of the other way around. Am I right?"

He smiled, then shrugged, neither admitting, or denying, what she said.

"Why?" she asked.

"Why what?"

"Why did you take such an interest?"

He paced across the room and peered out through the front blinds, seeing nothing in particular. "What are you trying to get me to say, Paige?"

She sat down her glass on the coffee table and went to him, standing a short distance away. "That you care."

He turned to her then. Their faces were close. "Oh, God, Paige. I care. I care too much. That...that's why I had to back away."

She touched a button of his blue dress shirt, the third button down, and her fingers scorched the skin beneath. "What is it, Zach? What are you afraid of?"

He stroked her hair softly, his fingers barely touching it. "Of loving you. Of...loving anyone."

"Because of Janet, because you lost her?"

"Yes." His word was sharp. One word, meant to make her stop, to make her back off.

It worked. She backed away as if he'd struck her. He hated that. He jerked her to him and kissed her hard, fiercely, selfishly, as if to rid himself of passion. His hands swam over her, touching her with greed and want until he heard her small cry. It stopped him as nothing could.

He released her, not wanting to hurt her. He'd never wanted to hurt her. But he knew he had, and would hurt her more if he didn't end things now for both of them.

"Sit down, Paige. You're right—we need to talk."

Paige took a seat on the sofa again, wanting to hear what Zach had to say, yet afraid to hear it, too. His rough kiss had awakened every nerve ending in her. She'd been both excited by it and frightened.

He paced the room in front of her, shoulders hunched, hands jammed into his pockets. He didn't speak for a while, as if he was gathering courage, and when he did, his voice was low, injured.

"Every day since Janet's accident, I've blamed myself," he said quietly. "It was just supposed to be a short trip to her parents' house, but it was raining that night. Janet hated to drive in the rain. I knew that—but I had a brief to prepare for court the next day. I let her go alone, alone with Jessie. . . ."

"There was a drunk driver. The roads were slick. Janet couldn't miss him. Maybe if I'd been driving, I could have—"

"Zach, you can't blame yourself for that. There was no way you could know there would be an accident," she interrupted, wanting to ease his guilt, the agony she heard in his voice.

"Maybe. Maybe not. But the fact remains, I didn't protect them. I wasn't there for Janet when . . . when she needed me. I didn't protect my family. Do you know what that does to a man, Paige?"

He'd turned to her, his eyes beseeching her to understand. And Paige thought that she did. She understood why he was so protective of Jessie, why he tried to shield her from hurt, real or imagined. Why he'd shaken in remembered fear that night he'd come to the hospital.

But she didn't know how to make it right for him again.

"I think I do know, Zach," she said softly. He was afraid to love her, to love anyone, this man who needed love himself, this man who had so much to give.

He stood in the middle of the room. She went to him, slid into his arms, uninvited. His heart thudded heavily in his chest. She wanted to absorb its beat, she wanted to absorb his pain.

If only she could.

"Paige, I don't want to hurt you, but I'm afraid I'll do just that. I'd smother you the way I do Jessie. You... you'd end up hating me. You'd end up leaving me the way you had to do with Stephen."

"Zach..."

At the moment she felt willing to risk every shred of independence she'd fought for and won. But what if Zach was right?

What if she ended up hating him? What if she brought him more pain? Him and Jessie?

"Paige, it has to be this way," he said, his voice barely recognizable. Then he leaned down and kissed her, a soft kiss, a gentle kiss.

A kiss of goodbye?

Chapter Ten

Zach worked alongside Paige, each of them acutely aware of the other. Zach was checking the lighting, and Paige was looking over his shoulder at every turn. Her soft, feminine fragrance curled around him and tormented his senses.

"Zach..."

"Yes?" He looked up and swallowed hard at her pale beauty in the theater light. Her cheeks were rouged lightly with excitement and her lips were full and pink. Would he ever be able to look at her and not have his breath catch in his throat? Would he ever be able to see her mouth pucker and not want to kiss it?

The answer that came to mind didn't please him.

"I just wanted to tell you that I numbered the scenery props in the order of the acts, and I lined up two other fathers to help you that night. Oh...and how are you coming on the mist for the third ballet number?''

"Don't worry, the third ballet number will have all the mist you need. There will also be clouds for the seventh number."

She hugged her arms to herself. "Of course ... I'm sorry. I just have a big case of preopening-night jitters, I guess."

A small frown creased her forehead. He wanted to kiss it away. "You're entitled. Why don't you try to relax and let me worry about the lighting and special effects, okay?"

"Relax? I don't think I know the meaning of the word. Well, you go on with whatever you were doing. I won't interrupt again." She turned and started across the stage to pester the sound man.

The old fellow was better equipped to deal with her rampant femininity than Zach was. *His* hormones had wheezed and died a number of years ago.

Zach gave a low groan and returned to the wiring he'd been working on.

Paige might not verbally interrupt him—at least for the next thirty minutes or so—but mentally she had him so that he could barely think. He tried to tell himself he'd made the right decision the other night, the *only* decision he could. But a thousand times a day, and many more during the long, restless nights, he wasn't so sure.

He wanted Paige, more than he wanted his next breath. And it was little comfort knowing that he'd made his decision as much for her sake as for his. All the altruism in the world wouldn't warm his bed at night.

Loving someone wasn't enough, though. That love—and the fear of losing that someone—would destroy them in the end. Besides, Paige wanted her independence, needed it to make her whole. He would take that from her in his attempt to protect the woman he loved.

He shoved the wires back inside the housing of the light he was checking and turned it on. Brilliance illuminated the stage. Colored sheets of heavy plastic, Paige called gels, gave the colored lighting effects she needed—red and yellow for warm hues, blue and purple for cool. The recital was an illusion, a chimera of light and fake mist and clouds.

And so was the way he and Paige had been treating each other the past few days. An act. And he hated it.

"That's it, everyone," Paige said a few hours later. "Dress rehearsal is in three days. I need you here for a run-through. And I can promise you chaos. All the dancers will be here, and for most of them, it will be their very first recital. So I'll need you to be patient. With them and with me."

Especially with me, Paige thought as she gave them a wide smile for their help. This was what she'd been working for, a part of her dream. And now that she had it in the palm of her hand, some of the glow had gone out of it.

Perhaps it was human nature to always want more.

She squeezed her eyes shut to keep from crying in front of her workers, in front of Zach, and raced to the back of the stage, behind the scenes, before the tears could flow.

Her dream was important, but she wanted Zach, too, *needed* him to make her life complete. She tried to tell herself a million times that he was right, everything he'd said the other night at his house was the truth. He would smother her, steal the very independence she'd been fighting for, and that she would end up hating him for it in the end.

Her independence. Maybe that was just another word for being alone. Alone, with no one to share things with—triumph and pain, laughter and tears.

All she knew was that she hurt, a deep-in-her-soul kind of hurt. She didn't know how she'd get through the rest of the week, working alongside Zach, close but unable to touch. She didn't know how she'd get through the rest of her life without him around at all.

And Jessie. The little girl had danced her way into Paige's heart. She loved her as much as if she were her own. Would Zach let his daughter continue her lessons? Perhaps he would—if Jessie wanted it.

But there would be no more casual outings for pizza. No more romantic evenings at the ballet in Kansas City. No more seeing Zach smile or hearing him laugh. No more kisses that tingled her toes and made her long for more.

"Everything's going well, don't you think?" Duncan asked, coming up behind her so silently she hadn't heard his approach.

She wanted to scream that no, everything was not all right and it never would be again. "Yes, Duncan, the show is shaping up just fine. In fact, there's not much left we can do here tonight. Why don't you lock up, and everyone can go home."

Maybe a run along the river would take her mind off it all, Paige thought as she gathered up her things and hurried out of the theater. She didn't glance in Zach's direction.

She had to get used to not seeing him in her life.

As Paige had predicted, dress rehearsal was chaotic. Ernestine had arrived with all the costumes and was busy pressing ruffles, taking tucks in at the waist or letting them out, adjusting straps or sewing on missing sequins.

The noise level was deafening. And added to it all was the sound man testing his equipment. Paige only hoped the squawks she heard emanating from the speakers would not be present on recital night.

What was the old saying? A poor dress rehearsal, a great opening show. Paige hoped it was true.

Zach and the two volunteer dads worked the scenery. The mist machine wouldn't mist and the clouds obscured the dancers instead of floating above them. The only favorable thing she could say about the rehearsal was that a tornado hadn't blown the dancers offstage.

"Whew!" Ernestine said, plunking her ample frame down on a sawhorse in the wings once the final act had swept offstage. "I see now that making all those costumes was the easy part of it."

Paige felt instantly sorry for her. Ernestine had taken on her task as wardrobe mistress without a word of complaint. Until now. "I brought a cooler of lemonade. Why don't I get us some?" Paige suggested.

"Lemonade? Sounds good."

Paige was back in two shakes with the cool drinks, but Ernestine was busily supervising the dancers as they took off their costumes.

"I'm not pressing them again on recital night," Ernestine barked. "If you don't hang them properly, you wear them wrinkled. Got that?"

Everyone got it. At least they all scurried for the hangers with their names on them.

Paige hid a smile. She could not have found a better wardrobe mistress if she'd scoured the earth for one. But—she remembered—Zach was the one who'd found Ernestine for her. Zach. She gave a small sigh. He was doing his part for the recital, giving one hundred percent and more, but she felt the distance between them, felt it keenly.

"I want to sit and enjoy this drink," Ernestine said, reaching for one of the glasses Paige was holding. She found a long bench backstage that looked more comfortable than the sawhorse and parked herself on it.

While the dancers were changing into their clothes and stuffing ballet and tap shoes into their dance bags, Paige joined her on the bench. "Thanks, Ernie, for everything. You're doing a great job," Paige said sincerely.

Ernestine grunted, uncomfortable with the compliment. "It'll be a good show," she said. "I can feel it in my bones."

"Well, let's hope your bones are on target this time," Paige returned.

"Hmmph! This old woman's not usually wrong about anything—*including* what's going on right under my nose."

Paige ducked her head and took a slow swallow of her drink. "What do you mean, Ernie?" She said it with such innocence, she should have considered an acting career.

"I mean, there's so much static electricity going on between you and Zach it's setting off sparks." She glanced up at the rafters. "And this is an old building."

Paige didn't feel like smiling at that. She didn't know if she'd ever smile again—and mean it. "Zach and I decided that...that things wouldn't work out for us," she said, hoping her fluff answer would be explanation enough.

But Ernestine was looking at her with a piercing eye that could rival a laser. "In any relationship there are things to work out. Whether or not you try depends on how strong the love is."

Ernestine's words stung like a hornet. How much did Paige love Zach? Enough to risk her independence? A fat lot of good that hard-won battle would do her when the winter winds blew down the Missouri and she found herself alone at night. Without Zach's kisses to warm her, without . . .

"Zach's not ready to risk loving anyone again, not now, maybe not ever," she said honestly to Ernestine.

This was private, between her and Zach, but the woman was like family. And she had eyes; she knew what went on in her house—and probably what went on in Zach's heart, as well.

"I say he's never going to find anyone better to risk loving than you. He needs a wife. And that little mite needs a mommy."

"Oh, Ernie, you're not playing fair, bringing Jessie into this." It was all she could do to consider Zach in this strange equation that was her life at present. Adding Jessie really complicated things. "I hope whatever happens between Zach and me won't affect my special friendship with her."

Paige glanced across the theater where Zach was dutifully tying the laces on Jessie's tennies, then he straightened and adjusted her perpetually crooked glasses. Paige had convinced her she looked pretty in them—and Jessie did. She was beautiful and precious and loving. Paige wanted the little girl in her life on a permanent basis.

And her daddy.

But she and Zach were poles apart.

"Well, I can tell you that if he was the man I loved, I wouldn't quit until I'd convinced him I was the best thing to come along since humans found fire," Ernestine went on like an unrelenting bulldog.

Paige watched as Zach took Jessie's hand in his. A lump rose in her throat, and she swallowed against it. "Oh, Ernie, I wish it were that easy."

"Daddy, can we go for pizza tonight?" Jessie asked, jumping up and down in front of him.

"Pizza, huh?" He knew Ernestine was worn to a frazzle from all the work she'd done lately on the costumes. Pizza would give her a break in the kitchen. "I suppose we could do that, sweetheart."

"Yeah! Can Paige come, too, can she please, Daddy?"

He'd known it would come to this sooner or later. He'd only hoped it would be later—and that he'd have an answer by then. He didn't. How did he make a four-year-old understand what a grown man couldn't get a handle on? That life wasn't simple and sometimes it stunk—like now.

"I thought it might be nice if just the two of us went. You can be my best girl."

Jessie cocked her head at him. "But Paige is your best girl."

The logic of a child. It could trip up heads of state.

He knew he would have to explain to Jessie, somehow, someway, that it was over between Paige and

him. Maybe tonight. After pizza. After he read her a
bedtime story. After...

There was no good time.

"Let's go see if Ernie wants us to bring her home an
order of that spaghetti she likes," he said, taking Jessie's hand.

A certain light went out of his daughter's eyes. She
loved Paige. That didn't make what he was going
through any easier, knowing Jessie would be hurt. It
was bad enough that he and Paige were walking
wounded.

He felt as if the sunshine had gone out of his life. So
many times the past few days he'd caught himself
about to pull Paige close, kiss her sweet mouth. He'd
wanted to touch her hair, her cheek. Each time he'd
stopped short of that, and each time the ache in him
had grown deeper.

At the pizzeria Zach placed their order, and Jessie
ran off to play. He watched her jump and climb, but
her usual exuberance was missing tonight.

He watched her to keep from thinking about Paige
and how she had looked sitting across from him. He'd
taken a different table tonight, but his mind refused to
be fooled.

He watched Jessie to assure himself nothing would
happen to her, his vigilance that hadn't missed Paige's
attention the first night they'd come here, that need of
his to protect his own, a need grown out of tragedy—
a need that stood between Paige and him.

He took a swallow of the beer he'd ordered but wasn't enjoying, then his gaze slid to Jessie. Was looking out for her such a crime?

She glanced over at him. The expression on her small face told him she was aware of his parental monitoring. He smiled, but she didn't return the gesture. Instead, she climbed down and paced across the room to him.

"Daddy," she said, her voice huffy, hands on hips. "I'm not a baby. You don't have to watch me."

Zach opened his mouth to say something, then closed it promptly. His gaze swept her face, those blue eyes that somehow seemed larger behind her glasses, the defiance of her stance, the same stance he'd seen in Paige more than once.

"I see," he said, leaning back in his seat. He looked everywhere but into the pierce of her eyes. Maybe he was afraid he'd see truth there.

Was Paige right? Was he smothering Jessie? Out of love? Out of fear? Would Jessie start to resent him, the way Paige had come to resent her father's smothering love?

Paige had been wronged—and he didn't want that for Jessie.

He drew in a sharp breath and let it out slowly.

"Come on, let's go see if our order's ready," he said to his daughter.

Jessie had given him a few things to think about.

* * *

The night had arrived. So had the butterflies in Paige's stomach—they were doing a serious tap dance, but she did her best to quell them.

In a few short hours the curtain would go up and her little darlings would dance their hearts out.

Backstage was abustle with activity. She knew she should be there, but she couldn't resist taking another moment to savor the quiet from third row, center. She'd been waiting for this night for months, planning for it down to the last detail, but that rush of excitement she'd expected to feel was conspicuously missing.

Accomplishments and goals were fine as far as they went, but they didn't bring happiness, not the total, blissful kind, the kind she knew she'd only find with Zach.

But Zach didn't want to risk his heart again. And he didn't want to risk hurting her. Strange, she thought, this really felt like hurting.

He hadn't arrived yet, but she knew she could count on him to be there. She could count on him to do his part to bring the show off. But when the curtain came down and the congratulations were over, he and Jessie would go back to their lives and she . . . she would go on with hers.

Somehow.

With a sigh she stood up from her seat, tucked her clipboard under her arm and edged her way toward the aisle.

"I wondered where you were."

The sound of the familiar male voice made her heart lurch. "Zach..."

He filled the aisle, looking more devastating than ever. His black knit shirt stretched across his broad shoulders, and his soft-faded jeans sheathed his lower body. The stage lights glistened in his hair, turning it as dark as a raven's wing. His eyes were shadowed as she tried to read them.

"All the action's backstage. What are you doing out here?" he asked with a nod at the empty theater.

She gave a faint smile. "I guess I was just trying to feel the excitement."

"And did you feel it?"

She didn't know what to say, didn't know how to tell him that the excitement wasn't there, not the way she'd expected it to be. "Maybe it'll come later. I still have a million things to do." She waved the clipboard for emphasis.

"Anything I can do to help?"

She shook her head. "No, you're already doing enough."

His gaze lingered on her for a moment. "Paige, the show will be fine."

"Will it? How do you know that?"

"Because I believe in you."

She squeezed her eyes shut. Next to hearing him say he loved her and wanted her, this was what she most needed to hear. She smiled, a soft, bittersweet smile. Bittersweet because of what she couldn't have. "I should be getting back,'' she said, as she tried to edge past him.

Zach stopped her with a gentle hand. Paige had never looked so soft, so feminine, as she did right now. She'd worn her hair in a long braid tonight, but several wisps had escaped and teased around her face.

She looked ethereal in her soft, drapey dress of pale green, ivory-colored ballet slippers on her feet. Her skin was pale white in the soft light, and there were traces of dark smudges beneath her eyes. She'd been working hard, too hard, trying to make this night magical for everyone concerned.

He reached out a hand to touch her cheek. He'd lost that right, but he had to feel the silk of it. He loved her—he knew that now. He couldn't live without her—he knew that, too. But he feared he'd blown his chance with her.

''I've missed you, Paige, so much that I ache inside.''

Paige didn't want to think about how much she missed him. She felt the same inside her. ''Zach, don't do this...''

He touched a trembling finger to her lower lip. ''Don't do what? Tell you how I feel? Tell you that I made the biggest mistake of my life by sending you away? Tell you that...I love you?''

He loved her? Paige took a small step back from the impact of those words. It was what she wanted to hear him say more than anything in the world, but she sucked in a breath, waiting for him to add the rest, that it couldn't be, that he couldn't allow her into his heart, into his life—and into Jessie's.

She looked away, not wanting him to see the tears she couldn't hold at bay. Why did he have to say these things tonight? Tonight, when she had so much at stake? If the recital was a flop, she'd find a way to live with that, but she didn't know how she'd live without Zach.

"Why are you saying these things?" she asked a tremor in her voice.

Zach tipped her chin up. "Why? Because I have to. I have to tell you that I want you, Paige. If...if you'll have me." If she didn't want him, he'd convince her, even if it took him forever. "Please say you love me and that you'll marry me."

"Marry?"

He heard the shock in her voice, saw the surprise in her eyes. All his hopes plummeted. He'd hurt her badly, and now she couldn't forgive him. "I'm sorry, Paige. I...I never meant to hurt you—and now I've upset you on the most important night of your life."

"Oh, Zach, you didn't upset me, you crazy, wonderful man. And you've just made this the most important night of my life, not the revue, but *you*. That's what's important to me. You—and Jessie."

She threw her arms around his neck and kissed him hard. He reveled in the taste of her, her softness, her passion. When he thought he could bear it no more, he drew back and looked into her eyes. "Is that a yes?" he asked, needing to hear the words.

"It's a very definite yes! Oh, Zach, I love you."

"Even if I'm possessive at times? If I am, it's only because I love you so fiercely."

"That's something Jessie and I intend to work on with you, and you might as well give in gracefully, big man."

"Is that right?"

"Yes, but I understand, Zach. I understand why you hold on so tightly to Jessie. You do it out of love, afraid that you'll lose her. But you won't lose her and you won't lose me. Ever."

He kissed her then, long and deep, certain he was drowning in her, and he never wanted to be rescued. He didn't release her until he heard Ernestine's booming voice.

"It would be nice if I could get a little work out of you two tonight," she said. "We have a recital to put on—in case you've forgotten."

Zach and Paige looked at her, then at each other, and began to laugh. "Shall we tell her now or after the show?" Zach asked.

"We need to tell Jessie, too," Paige returned. She thought for a moment. Jessie would be so excited she'd get all tangled in her own feet. "If we can hide these smiles on our faces, I think we'd better tell them both *after*."

"That, woman, is a tall order, given the way you make me feel."

They were able to keep their secret for about five minutes, then the whole cast knew. Jessie ran to her and threw her arms around her, then her daddy. "Paige is going to come live with us and be my new mommy?" she wanted to know.

"Would you like that, Jessie?" Paige asked her.

"Oh, yes!"

Ernestine even broke out a smile for the occasion. "I knew you two would work out your differences," she said, as if she possessed all the wisdom of the world.

And maybe she did.

That night when the curtain went up and Paige's little Broadway babies tapped their way across the stage, Zach slipped an arm around her shoulders and she knew it was the beginning of a wonderful life together.

"Wanna fool around with the stagehand?" he asked with a wicked smile.

"After the show," she promised. "And every night after that."

* * * * *

WHERE THE HEART IS

Get set for an exciting new series from
bestselling author

ELIZABETH AUGUST

Join us for the first book:

THE FORGOTTEN HUSBAND

Amnesia kept Eloise from knowing the real reason she'd
married cold, distant Jonah Tavish. But brief moments of sweet
passion kept her searching for the truth. Can anyone help Eloise
and Jonah rediscover love?

Meet Sarah Orman in *WHERE THE HEART IS.* She has a way
of showing up just when people need her most. And with her
wit and down-to-earth charm, she brings couples together—
for keeps.

Available in July, only from

Take 4 bestselling love stories FREE

Plus get a FREE surprise gift!

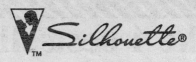

WILD RIVER

by
Laurie Paige

Maddening men...winsome women...and the untamed land they live in—
all add up to love! Meet them in these books from Silhouette Special Edition
and Silhouette Romance:

WILD IS THE WIND (Silhouette Special Edition #887, May)
Rafe Barrett retreated to his mountain resort to escape his dangerous feelings
for Genny McBride...but when she returned, ready to pick up where they
left off, would Rafe throw caution to the wind?

A ROGUE'S HEART (Silhouette Romance #1013, June)
Returning to his boyhood home brought Gabe Deveraux face-to-face
with ghosts of the past—and directly into the arms of sweet and loving
Whitney Campbell....

A RIVER TO CROSS (Silhouette Special Edition #910, September)
Sheriff Shane Macklin knew there was more to "town outsider"
Tina Henderson than met the eye. He saw a generous and selfless woman
whose true colors held the promise of love....

Don't miss these latest Wild River tales from Silhouette Special Edition
and Silhouette Romance!

SEWR-4

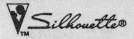

It's our 1000th
Silhouette Romance™,
and we're celebrating!

And to say "THANK YOU" to our wonderful readers, we would
like to send you a

FREE AUSTRIAN CRYSTAL BRACELET

This special bracelet truly captures the spirit of CELEBRATION
1000! and is a stunning complement to any outfit! And it can be
yours FREE just for enjoying SILHOUETTE ROMANCE™.

FREE GIFT OFFER

To receive your free gift, complete the certificate according to
directions. Be certain to enclose the required number of proofs-
of-purchase. Requests must be received no later than August 31,
1994. Please allow 6 to 8 weeks for receipt of order. Offer good
while quantities of gifts last. Offer good in U.S. and Canada only.

And that's not all! Readers can also enter our...

CELEBRATION 1000! SWEEPSTAKES

*In honor of our 1000th SILHOUETTE ROMANCE™, we'd
like to award $1000 to a lucky reader!*

As an added value every time you send in a completed offer
certificate with the correct amount of proofs-of-purchase, your
name will automatically be entered in our CELEBRATION 1000!
Sweepstakes. The sweepstakes features a grand prize of $1000.
PLUS, 1000 runner-up prizes of a FREE SILHOUETTE
ROMANCE™, autographed by one of CELEBRATION 1000!'s
special featured authors will be awarded. These volumes are sure
to be cherished for years to come, a true commemorative
keepsake.

DON'T MISS YOUR OPPORTUNITY TO WIN! ENTER NOW!

CELOFFER

CELEBRATION 1000! FREE GIFT OFFER

<u>ORDER INFORMATION:</u>

To receive your free AUSTRIAN CRYSTAL BRACELET, send three original proof-of-purchase coupons from any SILHOUETTE ROMANCE™ title published in April through July 1994 with the Free Gift Certificate completed, plus $1.75 for postage and handling (check or money order—please do not send cash) payable to Silhouette Books CELEBRATION 1000! Offer. Hurry! Quantities are limited.

FREE GIFT CERTIFICATE   096 KBM

Name:_____

Address:_____

City:_____ State/Prov.:_____ Zip/Postal:_____

Mail this certificate, three proofs-of-purchase and check or money order to CELEBRATION 1000! Offer, Silhouette Books, 3010 Walden Avenue, P.O. Box 9057, Buffalo, NY 14269-9057 *or* P.O. Box 622, Fort Erie, Ontario L2A 5X3. Please allow 4-6 weeks for delivery. Offer expires August 31, 1994.

PLUS

Every time you submit a completed certificate with the correct number of proofs-of-purchase, you are automatically entered in our CELEBRATION 1000! SWEEPSTAKES to win the GRAND PRIZE of $1000 CASH! PLUS, 1000 runner-up prizes of a FREE Silhouette Romance™, autographed by one of CELEBRATION 1000!'s special featured authors, will be awarded. No purchase or obligation necessary to enter. See below for alternate means of entry and how to obtain complete sweepstakes rules.

CELEBRATION 1000! SWEEPSTAKES
NO PURCHASE OR OBLIGATION NECESSARY TO ENTER

You may enter the sweepstakes without taking advantage of the CELEBRATION 1000! FREE GIFT OFFER by hand-printing on a 3" x 5" card (mechanical reproductions are not acceptable) your name and address and mailing it to: CELEBRATION 1000! Sweepstakes, P.O. Box 9057, Buffalo, NY 14269-9057 *or* P.O. Box 622, Fort Erie, Ontario L2A 5X3. Limit: one entry per envelope. Entries must be sent via First Class mail and be received no later than August 31, 1994. No liability is assumed for lost, late or misdirected mail.

Sweepstakes is open to residents of the U.S. (except Puerto Rico) and Canada, 18 years of age or older. All federal, state, provincial, municipal and local laws apply. Offer void wherever prohibited by law. Odds of winning dependent on the number of entries received. For complete rules, send a self-addressed, stamped envelope to: CELEBRATION 1000! Rules, P.O. Box 4200, Blair, NE 68009.

 ONE PROOF OF PURCHASE

096KBM

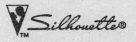

In 1993, Silhouette Romance held a FATHER OF THE
YEAR Contest. From the many wonderful entries that
we received, JOSEPH COSTANZO was chosen as the
Silhouette Romance "Fabulous Father" for 1993!

And here is his daughter Cathy's winning letter....

*"Dad was never the type of man who would bring home a
dozen store-bought, long-stemmed roses for Mom. But I'll
never forget the look on his face when he visited the flower
garden after a long day working construction jobs. He'd
take out his ever-present pocket knife and carefully trim
the thorns away before handing them over unceremonious-
ly to my mother with a boyish smile. Then he'd quickly
change the subject.*

*"Raising three daughters wasn't easy for this hardworking
man, especially the middle child. I stuck to him like glue.
I climbed pear trees when he told me he needed my help
gathering ripe pears. I shoveled chicken manure right by
his side when we fertilized the garden, and I watched in
awe as he built beautiful walls made of stone or brick. He
always made me feel so special. If I handed him a tool,
he'd thank me with his eyes, made me know I was
important. He never had to say how proud he was of me;
it was always there in his eyes. I wonder if he knows the
same pride and admiration is mirrored in my eyes
when I look at him."*

Cathy Giordano

FFLETT